FALLEN

THE
BLACK
MOON

SUNITA WHEELAN

Illustrated by Ignis Fatuus

Typography by May Dawney Designs

Published in 2020 by Sunita Wheelan

ISBN: 9798578632143
Imprint: Independently published

CONTENTS

Chapter One: The House of Rune

I struggled to sleep that night as I lay sprawled out on an aged, hard mattress, allowing the unfamiliar surroundings to consume me. The thin curtains allowed enough moonlight to pour through, casting an eerie shadow against the vintage wardrobe. A bucket had been placed in the corner of the room to catch the small droplets of water that fell, disturbing the silence with a rhythmic echo.

It had only been a few days since I'd moved to Willow Creek; a town I had never stepped foot in but was perfectly located far away from home, Sanctus Terra.

I had no friends in Willow Creek and little money left to my name. After my home was repossessed, I managed to secure myself a job as a maid, which I was due to begin the following morning. I knew it wasn't exactly the most glamorous job for a twenty-four-year-old, but I had to earn. Luckily, the owner of the property, Mr Dimitri Rune, was offering quite an attractive sum of money, along with in-house residency. An offer I couldn't refuse.

The job was given to me almost immediately after a brief telephone interview. As Mr Rune sounded like a no-nonsense kind of man, I thought it probably wise to save any embarrassing jokes for another time, in an attempt to break the ice. After advising of the many cleaning duties I would have (which I didn't understand how there could possibly be so many), Mr Rune had mentioned that he lived with just his three sons. A wave of anxiety had swept over me for a moment upon hearing this; however, I chose to ignore it. If only I had listened to my gut feeling.

I had finally drifted off to sleep when, before I knew it, dawn was upon me and the sun's rays seeped through a hole in the curtains. After a brisk shower and rushing to get dressed into a mid-length, black dress, I brushed my long brunette hair into a neat bun. I stared at the young woman looking back at me in the mirror, and my gaze fell upon the round silver locket that dangled around my neck. I opened it and longingly stared at the photo of my parents. I had my father's smile and my mother's spirit.

Today brings a new beginning and hope, I thought to myself as I kissed the photo with a heavy heart.

After applying minimal makeup to my sun-kissed skin and packing what little belongings I had, I sped down the stairs of the little B&B and out into the warm open air, where I was expecting my taxi to be waiting. What I was not expecting was a chauffeur waiting to take me to Mr Rune's residence in a beautiful, black Rolls Royce.

"Miss Stone?" the old man asked in a calm, unsteady tone.

"Err, yes . . . That's me."

"My name is Uriel. I have been sent by Mr Rune to collect you." He opened the door to the vehicle. "Please, allow me." As I eagerly hopped in, questions began to circle my mind. Was this family rich? How big was this house? Who exactly did I even agree to work for? Is it safe?

It's a tad bit late to ask that last question now, Sophia, I thought.

The journey to the house was silent as Uriel never uttered another word. I was occupied with looking out of the window, admiring the beautiful green lands we had driven past, eagerly awaiting our halt. Ten minutes later, but what had seemed like a lifetime of anticipation, we arrived at the gates to the entrance, and my jaw fell to the floor as I let out a gasp. As the tall, black iron gates opened of their own accord, I was captivated by what I saw ahead of me.

The straight, autumn-gold gravel path surrounded by emerald blades of freshly cut grass and immaculately trimmed sphere shrubs led us to the house. Only, this was not the kind of house I had imagined it to be. This was a mansion. A frightfully beautiful mansion made of beige and dark grey stone, measuring almost a hundred feet tall. Five jets of water sprayed into the air and glistened in the sun as it danced back down onto the round marble water fountain. A row of apple trees stood proudly, with each apple glistening like little red rubies in the sun.

A few wide central stone steps led me up to the front porch before I came to a stop. I tilted my head back, looking up at the two black, double doors standing in front of me. I looked behind me to see Uriel driving away, leaving me feeling abandoned and hesitant. My eyes rested on the overly large, brass door handles for a moment.

"Well, it's not exactly going to open itself," I muttered.

The palms of my hands began to sweat as I continued to glare at the door handle with a furrowed brow. I slowly reached towards to knocker before hesitating.

"Get a grip, Sophia, you can do this," I chanted to myself, yet my words seemed to have little impact. "It's just a great, big old house after all, with what seems to be very rich people . . . Possibly powerful people . . . Who wouldn't hesitate to fire you if you didn't polish their bedside table. OH MY GOD, I am going to get fired!"

As I began to delve into an anxious cycle, the doors burst open and there stood a pleasant-looking, middle-aged man with an inviting smile on the other side. His six-foot frame towered over my small stature as a gentle breeze danced through his glossy, black, shoulder-length hair. As he held out his hand to shake mine, his fitted green jumper shuffled over his well-maintained physique. A pair of reading glasses balanced on the end of his pointy nose, emphasizing his sparkling blue eyes.

"Sophia Stone." He smiled. "I am Dimitri Rune. Come in, come in. I trust the journey was short and sweet?"

"Yes, it was quite a pleasant jour . . ." I paused as I began to take in the surroundings.

It was mesmerizing.

The ceiling of the hallway hung with a grand champaign-crystal chandelier. The black wooden flooring was laid with a large, gold rug that had beautiful red intricate detail. Gold-framed paintings hung from the walls of what appeared to be angels. Yet the main feature of the hallway was its grand, mahogany staircase, which steered off both left and right.

The room was dimly lit, and as stunning as it appeared, I couldn't seem to shake the eerie chill running up my spine, as though something was wrong.

"Takes your breath away, doesn't it?" Mr Rune snapped me back to reality.

"It really does," I gasped.

"Well, it's your home now, too. Come. Let me give you a tour of the house and show you to your room."

After what seemed like fifteen minutes of being shown every room along the way, we arrived at my room. It was a room I never imagined I would have. A room fit for a princess. The queen-sized bed was dressed in champaign silk covers, and a small, elegant chandelier hung low from the ceiling above the round, beige rug at the foot of the bed. A white marble dressing table sat in front of the window, where the sun poured through.

The room had a bright and inviting presence about it. It almost made me feel safe.

"I hope this is to your liking, Miss Stone?" Mr Rune was stood at the door, watching me with a smile.

My face was lit up with joy. "I've only read about these sorts of rooms in fairy tales. I grew up in a small cottage, you see. We never had such luxuries. But I feel like this is all a crazy dream."

"I can assure you this is all very much real. We are fortunate to have all that we have. I feel you will settle in here very well." He nodded as he passed a reassuring wink.

He continued to show me around the rest of the mansion, talking through my list of duties that were due to commence the following morning.

". . . Plants need to be watered, furniture needs polishing, paintings need dusting, bedrooms need attending . . ."

Mr Rune's words suddenly seemed to drown out as my eyes shifted to one room he seemed to miss out. The door to this room was aged with stress and cracks, and far darker in colour compared to the other doors in the house.

"Oh, that room always remains shut," he added, noticing I had become distracted. "There is nothing of interest in there. It's just a small storage room. You won't be able to get in, as I keep it locked. It's unnecessary. So, don't worry, it's not on your list of duties."

Strange. Why keep an old storage room locked if it's not of any importance. Almost as if it's . . . secret.

Before I could question him further, however, the frown that had appeared across my forehead melted away as two young men appeared out from around the corner.

"Well, you must be Sophia," said the blonde-haired man who was just as tall as his father. His golden hair was combed neatly away from his fresh-looking face, and his dazzling blue eyes smiled back at me. "My name's Vlad, and this is my brother, Rogue," he confirmed as he pointed to his brunette-haired brother.

My eyes shifted to Rogue. Without realising, I began to scan his tall, well-maintained physique slowly until I caught his espresso eyes watching me. Noticing the smirk Rogue was now wearing, I quickly adjusted myself. There was no doubt these two were clearly two of Mr Rune's sons, with attractive genes that clearly ran in the family.

"Father, can I speak with you for a moment?" Vlad gestured around the corner, and the two left.

"Must feel strange, no? Coming to a house as big as this with complete strangers residing within its walls?" said Rogue as he gestured me to walk with him.

"It's an unusual feeling, but then again, I find it quite exciting. I mean, a new place, a new job, and hopefully new friends."

"If you ask me, it sounds like you're running away from something. You can't run away from the past, Sophia. Everything happens for a reason."

I whipped my head around to meet his steel gaze and crossed my arms over my chest. "Who said I was running away from anything?"

Rogue laughed. "Woah woah, no need to get so defensive."

"I wasn't. I'm not," I lied.

"If you say so." He smiled.

Whenever he smiled, his eyes tended to do the same. For some reason, it was comforting. I didn't know him at all, yet I could trust him.

"Mr Rune mentioned you had another brother?" I said in an attempt to change the subject.

"Yes. Adrian. He will be arriving tonight. He is out on some . . . business. However, I feel I should warn you. He isn't like the rest of us."

"What do you mean?"

"Let's just say, he doesn't like being told what to do. We're not really close. He's selfish, rude, and, even though he is my blood, I wouldn't trust him. But you can trust me." He gave me another warm smile.

For some reason, after hearing about Adrian, the same uneasiness I had felt earlier crept through me, and it most definitely didn't leave me feeling safe.

Chapter 2: Adrian

It was 11.45 pm, and as nice as the silk bed sheets felt on my skin, I just couldn't sleep. I must have tossed and turned about ten times in the space of two minutes. I got out of bed and opened the latch on the window in hopes of getting a cool breeze, but the air was still. I couldn't feel the slightest draft, just peaceful sounds that echoed from the water fountain outside.

As I stared out into the night, I thought I saw a dark shadow moving behind the trees from the corner of my eye. I stared harder for a few moments, but I couldn't see anything. My restless eyes were clearly playing tricks on me.

Why would there be anyone lurking behind the trees?

As the room began to fill with the sound of my belly rumbling, I walked to the kitchen for a midnight snack. I opened the tall fridge and was pleasantly surprised to find it full of all sorts of delicious foods and treats. I reached to grab the bowl full of strawberries.

"You know, just because you were lucky enough to be given a job here, does not mean you can steal whatever you want, girl," said a slow, deep voice.

I shrieked and almost dropped the bowl. I turned to find a tall figure in the shadow. "I . . . I was just hungry, so I —"

I stopped as he began to move closer without faltering his stern gaze until he was mere inches from my face.

The moonlight peered from the window and poured through his bouffant, black hair and onto his face. His beautiful dark brown eyes pierced into mine, and my heart skipped a beat. He wore a black, skin-tight T-shirt over his broad, robust figure. His muscles bulged as he moved to rest his arm on the fridge above my head.

He looked me up and down with a sinister grin on his face. "You look juicy enough to eat. What if I decide to rip you apart right now, limb from limb and devour every inch of you?"

I pursed my lips while resisting the urge to run as far away from him as possible.

"Do I scare you, girl? Then again, I wouldn't want a nasty aftertaste in my mouth," he spat.

"If that's your attempt to scare me, Adrian Rune, you really ought to work on your technique more," I snarled back as anger brewed in my throat. "My name is *Sophia*, not *girl*! And if you didn't know, Mr Rune has given me residency here, so as far as you're concerned, this is my home as well as my job."

Adrian continued to stare at me with his hateful, beautiful eyes for a moment before opening his mouth again. "This may well be your *home* . . . for now, but you won't be calling it that for long. Not if I have anything to do with it." On that note, he drifted off into the dark hallway.

I stormed back up the stairs on an empty stomach with furrowed brows and a sharp lump in my throat. My heart was beating faster than normal. Anger still raged inside of me, but I knew I needed to gain control. I couldn't risk losing my job.

As I got to my room, I swung the door shut and locked it, just to be on the safe side, before throwing myself onto my bed.

How could someone hate somebody so much without knowing anything about them? Rogue said he couldn't be trusted. But if he was dangerous, then why would he still be living here? Surely Mr Rune wouldn't allow it.

After a few moments, my anger distinguished, curiosity taking its place, but as I tried to go back to sleep, all I kept seeing was Adrian's face every time I closed my eyes, sparking that familiar spurt of anger.

Urghh, this is going to be such a long night.

The morning finally dawned, and I felt as though I had only slept a few hours. It was eight am and no one seemed to be awake, the house filled with a strange silence.

After freshening up and getting dressed in my basic black uniform, I made my way down the hallway. I began polishing the ornaments displayed on the cabinet, most of which seemed strange, even for a mansion like this. There were some beast-like looking creatures, ones I'd never seen before in any books I had read. Yet they were sat upright as humans would. The Runes also seemed to love pentagon-shaped objects, as they had many of these lying around. The paintings on the walls looked even more unusual: One painting showed a group of people circled around a baby in the night. Another showed a child in what looked like a dark pool of water, smiling, yet there was something sinister about it. Another pictured two magnificent double doors with intricate engravings of serpents.

These signs should have rung alarm bells at that point, but unfortunately, it didn't; instead, a strange shiver rode up my spine, and the next thing I heard was a huge bang from one of the rooms above, making me jump.

"What the hell was that?"

Panicking, thinking someone may have hurt themselves, I ran up the stairs to see what it was. As I reached the top step, I heard a second bang, which directed me to where the sound was coming from: the last room at the end of the narrow corridor. Adrian's room.

For a moment, I began to turn back around. I really didn't need to spoil my morning. But after a third bang, I ran to the bedroom door, where I stopped and hesitated for a moment. My heart began to beat faster. I had no clue what was behind this door, or if Adrian was even inside. My palms began to sweat. I took a deep breath and turned the brass doorknob with a shaking hand. There was a trail of clothes, shoes, empty alcohol bottles and paperwork scattered on the floor that lead to the ruffled, occupied bed, where Adrian lay topless with two naked women, who were both kissing him as though they were feasting on meat.

Adrian locked eyes with me after noticing I was in the room, and a malicious smile crossed his face.

"Oh hey 'girl'. Come to watch the show have we, or did you feel left out?" he smirked.

I rolled my eyes, knowing I had just wasted my time. "No thanks. I only came to see what all the noise was. Now that I've seen, I'll try my best to wash my eyes out," I fired back before turning to leave.

"Wait. I'm sorry," he called back.

I stopped and turned to face him as lines began to appear across my forehead.

The smirk had vanished from his face. "Ladies, where are my manners. Allow me to introduce you to Sophia," he announced, stretching out his arm towards me. "She is in fact a highly talented young woman and a new member of our family. You see, when I first met Sophia, I misjudged her. I thought she would just be a useless burden with nothing about her. I was wrong. She is neither useless nor a burden." He smiled.

I continued to stare into his eyes with disbelief, feeling taken aback.

Maybe I was wrong about him. Maybe Rogue was wrong about him. But why the sudden change of heart?

"She has many impressive skills," he continued. "For instance, if I throw this plate of leftovers on the floor like so, she will have to clean it up like the good little servant girl she is," he spat back as he tossed the plate on the hard flooring, shattering it to pieces. His sinister smirk had now returned.

I pursed my lips, and my hands were clenched into fists. Rage brewed at my throat, threatening to explode out of my body.

"Sophia here is like our family pet. If I snap my fingers, she will have to obey my every command if she is to remain here. She is not useless. She is pathetic. A waste of space, a pitiful creature. Yet we have been so kind and generous to have given her a roof over her head and a job she does not even deserve. No matter, though. If my pet disobeys me, I may have to . . . teach her a lesson." His eyes ripped into mine as though I were his worst enemy. "Come, slave, clear up this mess." He snapped his fingers and pointed to the shattered china.

The two women cackled, as though they were watching the most amusing show they had ever seen.

I had never felt so humiliated in my life. I stood there in silence, without drifting my gaze away from his eyes. I never thought I could hate someone as much as I hated him. In that moment, I really did feel like nothing. Belittled and a failure. My clenched fists surrendered and became limp beside my body. I tried hard to fight back the tears so as to not give him any satisfaction.

I knew that he could get me fired at any given moment, and I had nowhere else to go, so I reluctantly shuffled forward to pick up the mess he had made until I heard a firm voice behind me.

"Sophia, stop," said Rogue as I turned to face him. He wore a frown and was glaring at Adrian with what appeared to be as much hatred as me.

"Leave, now." He pointed towards the two women, who immediately got up, grabbed their belongings and ran out the room. "I will not allow you to treat her that way, Adrian. She is not your toy to play with or humiliate," he ordered.

"Dear brother!" shouted Adrian as he got up and walked towards him, still shirtless. "Always around to spoil all the fun, aren't you? We both know you don't care for the girl, so why don't you run along to Father and stay out of my business," he shot back as he placed a firm hand on Rogue's shoulder.

Rogue swiftly brushed his hand away. "Oh, I care more than you think."

"Hahaha. Oh, come on," Adrian said, mere inches from his face. "We both know what it is you really want from her." He leaned in closer and whispered, "Father would be proud," before leaving the room smiling.

"Are you all right?" asked Rogue as he turned to look back at me, his face full of concern. "Don't let him get to you. I did warn you that he would be like this. I regret having him as my brother, but mostly I just pity the fool." He moved closer and wiped the tears, which I had now allowed to fall down my blushing face. "As long as I am around, you have nothing to fear." He smiled.

I smiled back at him. I wouldn't have known what to do if I didn't have Rogue there to cheer me up. I felt safe when he was around. I felt . . . at home.

Yet what did Adrian mean by 'Father would be proud'?

Chapter 3: The Locked Room

If ever there was a time when you could slice the tense atmosphere with a blade, this would be that moment. Mr Rune seemed to think it would be a great idea to have an evening sit down meal with his sons, Uriel and me. But I thought otherwise.

As well as being a chauffeur, Uriel was also the household cook. The large mahogany table was laid with the finest silver cutlery, goblets of red wine and mouth-watering dishes. Delicious aromas filled the dimly lit dining room while steam from the hot, succulent roast danced in the candlelight. Yet both the ambience and my appetite were completely ruined by the presence of Adrian, who sat opposite me, glaring. He was just as ugly on the inside as he was beautiful on the outside.

"Sophia, how are you finding your new home? I hope that we have done justice in making you feel comfortable here," asked Mr Rune, breaking the silence.

I glanced back at Adrian, who was still glaring at me with a poker face.

"I love it here. I feel so at home, and you have all been so kind to me . . . especially Adrian," I half-lied, staring right back at Adrian with a false smile.

I could see Rogue smirking beside me from the corner of my eye.

"Oh, I assure you, there is so much more kindness to offer," uttered Adrian.

"Believe me, I intend to repay the favour." That familiar anger slowly returned to my throat as my sentence ended in a snap. I swear it had almost made him wince.

Adrian didn't respond but continued to scowl through squinted eyes.

There was only so much longer I could continue the act of not being intimidated by his piercing gaze. Truth be told, I was drawn to his beauty . . . And I hated that.

"I'm glad all is well. It is nice to have a female presence in the house," interrupted Mr Rune, who had noticed the staring competition going on but had chosen to ignore it

"I, erm, couldn't help but wonder, but, where is Mrs Rune?" I asked with a knitted brow. Of course, the thought had crossed my mind a few times, but I wasn't sure if it was the right time or the right thing to ask.

There was an awkward silence for a moment as I looked around at everyone.

Mr Rune had frozen midway from eating the meat off his fork, Rogue continued to stare at his half-eaten beef pie, Vlad and Uriel were suspiciously glancing at one another, and Adrian continued to tear the chicken off the bone without being fazed.

"She . . . unfortunately passed away," said Mr Rune slowly. "But that was a long time ago."

"Oh, I'm . . . I'm sorry. May I ask how did she die?"

"Disease," confirmed Vlad.

"Cancer, to be precise," Rogue added.

I glanced at Adrian opposite me, who had since stopped stuffing his face with food and was no longer glaring at me. Instead, he was staring at Rogue. Something didn't quite seem to add up. Since moving into the mansion, I had polished nearly all of the paintings in the house. Yet I did not come across a single photo of the Runes, let alone Mrs Rune.

"Oh, I almost forgot, I have an offer for you, Sophia. Something you may find appealing," said Mr Rune, swiftly changing the subject. My suspicious thoughts dissolved as I looked at him, intrigued. "Do you like to read?" he went on.

"I love to read. When I have the time, that is."

"How would you like to leave your cleaning duties behind and instead look after our Library?"

"Oh, that would be lovely!" My eyes lit up, and a wide smile spread across my face. As grateful as I was to be given an opportunity as a maid, cleaning the mansion was definitely not a one-person job.

"Good! Then it's settled. I will find someone else to fill your position as our maid. The library is yours from now on to look after, and I will, of course, continue to pay your wages. If there is anything you need, you can come to me." He grinned.

"Well, it has been a *wonderful* family meal," said Adrian as he stood up. "Uriel, epic roast, as always," he continued, winking at Uriel, who remained straight-faced.

"Before you run away, Adrian, I need a word." Mr Rune left the room as Adrian dragged his feet, following him outside.

"Sophia, some of our friends will be throwing a house party tomorrow night," said Vlad, bringing my attention back to the room. "We would love for you to come along, assuming you don't have any plans for Saturday, that is?"

"Nope, she has no plans. She will come," Rogue said, smiling.

"Thank you for speaking on my behalf, although I am perfectly capable of speaking for myself," I shot back before quickly forgiving his cheeky comment.

My mother had never allowed me to attend any parties with my friends. Being a single parent, she was always so overprotective. I resented her for it at the time, never understanding why I couldn't have a life like other friends, but now, I would do anything to be able to see her again.

"You ok, Sophia?" asked Rogue, snapping me back to the present.

"Sorry, yes. A party sounds great. I, erm, just have one small issue. I don't have anything to wear. I mean, I have clothes, of course, but nothing to suit the occasion."

"Well, looks like a shopping spree is in need," said Vlad.

"I would happily take you tomorrow, but we are all away on business during the day. Raven will take you. She's a friend of mine. I will arrange for Uriel to take you into town to meet her," said Rouge.

"Sounds great!" In truth, I was more excited about finally having some female company than outfit shopping. Who knows, maybe Raven and I might get along well.

After feeling overly full and exhausted, I climbed the stairs with great effort, looking forward to a good night's sleep. Upon reaching the top step, however, I heard a strange noise. It almost sounded like glass shattering from around the corridor to my right. I turned the corner to find nothing but a rusted door. The storage room. Thinking I must have imagined it, I turned to head back to my room, until the sounds of what appeared to be hissing stopped me. It was coming from the storage room.

But how could that be if the room is both empty and locked? Then I heard it.

"Sssophia," it hissed.

Shivers raced down my spine, yet at the same time, I felt compelled to move towards the door.

"Sssophia . . . Sssophia," it continued.

The closer I edged towards the door, the faster it hissed my name. I was merely inches from reaching the door handle, my hand shaking, heart pounding fast, when a familiar voice behind me made me jump out of my skin.

"Sophia?" called Rogue.

"Rogue did . . . did you hear that?" I asked, frightened.

"Hear what? I don't hear anything," He looked confused.

The voice had vanished as quickly as it had appeared. There was nothing but complete silence.

"I swear I heard a noise coming from that room. It was hissing my name!" I told him.

"Wait, *hissing* your name? Are you trying to tell me that a snake has somehow found its way into the locked room and can also communicate with humans?" said Rogue, looking rather amused.

"No, but I . . . I mean . . . When you say it like that, I know it sounds crazy, but . . ."

"Listen, you're obviously really tired." He placed a reassuring hand on my shoulder.

"Yeah, you're right. I think I'll go to bed. Thanks, Rogue." I smiled before walking away.

But . . . I swear I heard that hissing.

I threw myself on to the bed as I got into my room, feeling distracted and drained, both mentally and physically. I closed my eyes and, within seconds, found myself drifting off to sleep.

I was back in Sanctus Terra where my mother and father were dining together. Father moved Mother's long, brunette hair away from her face as he looked at her in admiration. They looked so happy together.

Everything became a blur, and then all of a sudden, we were in a hospital with Mother and Father sat in an office with a doctor.

"What are you saying, Dr Jones?" asked Mother, who was clearly disturbed.

"I am really sorry to have to tell you this, Ana, but you are infertile. Unfortunately, you will not be able to have children," Dr Jones explained.

Mother burst into tears whilst father embraced her.

Everything became a blur again, and I was back at the mansion, lying on my bed, with a dark figure over me, thrusting between my legs back and forth, both of us in a pool of sweat. My hands ran up his back and held on to his broad shoulders as he devoured my lips. My senses were heightened as a heated pulse spread between my legs. All I knew at that moment was how much I wanted him. I wanted all of him.

Chapter 4: A Night to Forget

The alarm buzzed loudly at nine am as I jolted upright, heart racing and drenched in sweat.

What a strange dream. Of course, it had to be a dream. My mother was clearly not infertile, or else I wouldn't be here today. My thoughts turned to the mysterious figure for a moment. *Being a virgin, I've never experienced that level of pleasure before, let alone in my fantasies. Yet . . . it felt so real.*

I watched as a flock of crows danced back and forth in the clear blue sky as Uriel drove me to meet Raven that morning. Willow Creek wasn't a huge town, but it was a busy town. Crowds of people shuffled through the packed stone streets decorated with colourful market stalls. Window displays ranged from extravagant merchandise to antique ornaments, and as I stepped out of the car, I was welcomed by the delicious aroma of freshly baked bread coming from the bakery behind me.

"So, you must be Sophia," said a female voice.

I spun and had my breath taken away by a beautiful figure standing before me. Her long blonde hair draped her slender back, a pair of tight-fitted blue jeans paired with a fitted black blouse hugged her figure, her lips rose red and her eyes were sapphire blue.

"Yep, that would be me," I said, smiling.

"You really are as beautiful as they say." She analysed me from head to toe with a furrowed brow, a critical expression crossed her face. She almost looked . . . upset. As though she had just realised I was watching her, she looked at me and grinned; although, it didn't seem as genuine as she intended.

"Oh, well thank—" I started before she cut in.

"So, you've also been invited to tonight's party. Excited?"

"Yeah . . . I'm looking forw—"

"Will Adrian be coming along?" she asked, interrupting me again with a glint of hope in her eyes.

"I hope not," I muttered, irritated by her rudeness and for reminding me of that devil.

"Hmm, shame. His company would have been useful," she said, lust dripping from her every word. "I'm sure there will be others for us to both play with." She chuckled.

"I mean . . . I'm honestly looking forward to making friends and . . ."

"Wow . . . you sound like a virgin." She sniggered until my silence confirmed it. "Oh my . . . you are a virgin!" she proclaimed. "So, it's true," she muttered to herself.

"Sorry?"

"Nothing. We better get going if we're going to find you something to wear."

She led the way with reluctance hesitating her every step, until we arrived at shop called *Madame.* It wasn't very big inside; however, the mannequins were dressed in rather glamourous outfits.

Raven wasted no time wandering off in search of the right dress, before returning minutes later with a dress way too short for my liking. "This one! This would look fab on you and will have men drooling."

It was a figure-hugging, fluorescent dress with the top half heavily embroidered. A flamingo came to mind as she waved it about in front of me.

"Erm, don't you think it's a bit short?"

"Urgh, that's something only a virgin would say. You're not planning on staying one forever, are you? I mean, it's a little embarrassing, if I'm honest."

My mouth was ajar and my eyebrows raised upon hearing that. It was bad enough that she knew I was a virgin, but sounding like I wanted to remain one just made it so much worse. "I am so up for losing my virginity!" I blurted out, sounded maybe a little too keen. "I'm just . . . I'm waiting for the right guy."

What's wrong with you, Sophia! The right guy? You couldn't have said something else? Anything else!

"Who? A prince on a white horse? Ha ha. Listen, hunny, there aren't any guys left out there like that. They're only in fairy tales. If you wait for the right person, you will be waiting forever. That's why I lost mine a while ago."

All I wanted to do in that moment was to get out of the shop and back home. I picked up the first dress that caught my eye and walked over to the young cashier to pay without saying a word.

"Really? You're going to wear that? It's a bit . . . basic," she said, looking unimpressed.

"Well, I guess that must be me then. Basic," I snapped, rolling my eyes as I began to lose my patience.

Back in my room, I rushed to slip into my new sky-blue dress as the wooden clock chimed eight pm. It *was* a beautiful dress, and yet tasteful at the same time. The fabric was cut from fine silk that fell just above my knees, whilst the delicate straps rested on my bare shoulders. The silver locket, which dangled around my neck, complemented the look. After setting my loose curls and painting my lips a dusty rose shade, I headed down the stairs. Only, I didn't get far down the steps before I froze as I spotted Adrian wandering across the hallway.

He glanced up, noticing me, and stopped in his tracks. He looked at me for a moment, but not with disgust. He almost had a look of awe about him. My heart started to beat faster, and I was preparing myself for insults to be thrown my way, yet he never uttered a word. After a few seconds, but what felt like minutes, he continued to walk across the hallway and out of sight.

"Wow, you look . . . amazing," whispered Rogue, who appeared at the foot of the staircase.

"Thanks." A blush crept across my face.

"Vlad is already at the party. Uriel is ready to drive us there. Let's go." He gestured me to follow him outside into the chilly evening air.

After fifteen minutes, we arrived at the house. It was no mansion, but was a fairly larger house than average where loud music echoed the dark streets as guests entered.

As I walked inside and looked around, I could see the party had an acquired taste. The house was full of people, and everyone was dressed in dark attire, matched by the vintage lamps lit in the corners of the walls, creating a dense ambience. One woman was entertaining a group of others with a cobra wrapped around her neck. Oddly, she seemed to be rather affectionate towards it, and surprisingly, it wasn't trying to sink its fangs into her face. As we moved farther along, there were some people making out in the corners of the room, and others were getting lost in the music as they danced as though under a trance. A slight discomfort began to reside within me, as one by one people stopped and turned my way as I walked by. As though I were fresh meat.

"Hey, I'll go and get us some drinks and look for Vlad whilst I'm at it. I'll be back in a second." Rogue smiled as he walked away.

Feeling awkward from the looks I continued to receive, I was even glad to see Raven approaching. She was walking beside a man who appeared to be eyeballing me. His styled, mousey blonde hair complemented his dazzling emerald eyes, whilst his white shirt shuffled over his slender body as he walked. His cheeky smile showed off his immaculate white teeth.

"Oh, so you showed up," Raven said, sounding disappointed. "Sophia, meet our host, Ink. Ink, meet—"

"Sophia Stone," Ink completed as he took my hand to kiss it, causing my cheeks to flush. "It is a pleasure to finally meet you. Welcome to my home."

"Thank you for having me."

He continued to stare at me for a moment with menacing eyes before reaching to grab two drinks off a tray from someone walking by. "It would almost be rude not to have a drink at my party. Tonight, is all about having fun." He winked as he handed Raven and me a drink.

Raven giggled as she gulped the whole content of her glass, whilst I simply managed to gulp down a quarter of mine. It tasted of liquorish, which felt warm as it swam down my throat. Within minutes, I felt my whole body relax as my eyes became heavier. I didn't know exactly what was in my glass, but I could tell it was strong.

"I would love to give you a tour of my home, if you would let me?" asked Ink, showing his dazzling teeth.

What do I say? I can't offend him by refusing. I'm a guest in his home. But then again, why do I have a feeling that this is a bad idea?

My eyes swiftly wandered about the room, hoping I would find Rogue, when the sounds of shrieking women bellowed from the living room.

"He's here!" screamed Raven as she jumped up and down, waving her arms frantically for a moment before running off towards the noise.

As I could still feel Ink's uncomfortable gaze on me, I decided to follow Raven.

The gloomily lit room with its plain black walls gave off an eerie vibe. A thick layer of cigar smoke lingered in the atmosphere, whilst warm lamps flickered in the corners of the room. Perched on the crimson leather sofa was Adrian, surrounded by drooling women.

Raven didn't hesitate to walk up to him. "You know, I'll be sleeping *alone* tonight . . . in a *cold* bed. Do you want to help me . . . warm it up?" She glided a fingertip up his broad chest.

A twinge of jealousy pricked my chest as I watched her, trying hard to ignore the feeling.

"Not tonight, Raven." He smiled, moving her hand away.

Raven looked as though she had just been slapped in the face with brutal force. "It's her, isn't it?" she asked after finding her breath again, pointing straight at me, with Adrian only just noticing I was present.

His body froze as his eyes fixated on me.

"You want her! Why? I can give you so much more! What's so special about her?"

"I assure you, if I had to choose between fucking her or a pig, I would gladly choose the pig. I do not desire the girl in any way. The sight of her even makes me want to vomit."

His words caused sniggers to echo through the room.

A smile spread across Raven's flushed face as she looked over at me with wide eyes.

Whether it was the anger that fuelled me or the alcohol taking over, I suddenly felt a wave of overwhelming confidence to step forward and speak my mind. "Do you know what I see when I look at you, *Adrian*?" I began as I continued to step closer towards him. "I see an ungrateful, spoiled little *boy*. A coward who takes joy in defaming women. A pitiful disgrace to your gender. You're not a real man. Real men treat women with respect. Deep down, you're just *pathetic* . . . and *weak*."

Silence surrounded the room as the music had been turned off whilst guests were watching.

Adrian's chest began to pump faster, a vein now appearing to throb in his temple. He jumped to his feet and grabbed my hair tightly, pulling my head back towards him. "I could show you how much of a man I am right here, right now in front of all these people. Whores like you are the scum of this world. You're only useful for one thing with the few brain cells you have. You don't deserve to be respected or loved by any man or woman. No one would ever want you, because they think you're special, but only to bed you if they're desperate." Hatred licked at his voice as he continued to grip onto my hair.

"Adrian . . ." said Raven, her voice surprisingly full of concern before he spoke over her.

"I heard your mother enjoyed opening her legs to a group of strangers. She would be proud of you if she were still alive. Like mother, like daughter. Oh well. At least there's one less vermin on the planet." He breathed heavily onto my face.

Tears streamed down my face. Every word of his pierced a wound in my heart. My mother was no whore. I knew who she was, and I refused to believe him. What I did believe was that I was never going to be loved or wanted by anyone in this dark, lonely world. I didn't feel beautiful or special.

There's no place for me at the Rune's. I was better off alone.

As my thoughts trailed off into the dark distance, Adrian's forehead began to soften, noticing the tears staining my burning cheeks. His grip immediately loosened as he let go of my hair,

"I think that's enough drama for one night. Back to the party everyone!" Ink shouted, breaking up the scene.

The music blared once again, and everyone returned to partying, but Adrian continued to look at me with knitted brows.

"Sophia, darling? Erm, how about that tour?" Ink asked, smiling.

Feeling hollow inside, I gulped downed the remaining three-quarters of my drink.

"Love to," I whispered, tears still falling. As I followed him out of the room, I could feel Adrian's eyes burning the back of my head.

As Ink led me upstairs, however, I suddenly didn't feel so good. As my knees became weak and my vision became blurred, Ink grabbed my arm just in time, saving me from falling down the stairs.

"Oh dear, you don't look too well. You need to sit down. Come this way." He threw open a bedroom door. I just about reached the large bed before the room began to spin. "You know, you have your mother's eyes. Big, beautiful brown eyes," Ink whispered, a hint of obsession in his voice.

"Wait . . . how do you know my—?"

"She asked for help once. Something . . . she couldn't go back on. But you . . . You are something *special*. Yet you have no idea how special you are, which makes this all so much more exciting." He cackled. He came closer and laid on the bed beside me. "You are the key to unlocking . . . something great."

I had no idea what he was talking about. All I could think about was how much I just wanted to sleep as my eyelids became heavier. I felt his cold fingers stroking my warm skin, causing goosebumps to appear.

"I don't see why *I* wasn't chosen when *I* am more than capable of fulfilling part of what is needed. Nonetheless, I will have you tonight," he sneered as he tore off my left shoulder strap.

"No . . . please!" My chest began to fill with dread as I screamed.

"Hmm . . . what a pretty necklace. I think I'll trade it in for something useful." He ripped it off my neck, then began to pull my legs wide apart.

"No, no please don't . . . I don't want to . . . I'm a virgin," I said, helplessly.

"That you are indeed, my beauty, but not after tonight." He began to climb on top of me.

BANG!

The door was broken in, and Ink was suddenly pulled back and pinned against the wall by a tall figure. I couldn't make out who it was, my vision so blurred it felt as if I were being sucked into a dark hole.

"What is your problem?" Ink choked.

"If you lay another filthy finger on her again, Incubus, I will tear out your intestines slowly and feed them to you."

"But I thought you . . ."

"Information only seems to go in one ear and out the other with you. Allow me to fix that," the voice whispered.

"Arghhh! My ear! You bit off my ear!"

"Take that as a warning. That is if you care to keep the rest of you intact."

"You dishonour him! The prophecy has already been written. The Lord knows all!" He dashed out of the room.

The figure crept towards me in silence. Strong arms wrapped beneath me as I was lifted off the bed and carried outside. I could smell his dark, musky cologne from his chest. I felt unusually safe in his tight grasp. I don't remember if he ever spoke, but everything became dark as I drifted off to sleep.

"Unfortunately, you are infertile. You will not be able to have children," Dr Jones explained.

Ana burst into tears whilst Carlos embraced her.

Everything became a blur, and I was now in a damp, dark alley. Ana was there talking to a hooded figure.

"And . . . you say this will work?" questioned Ana, who looked puzzled.

"Yes," said the mysterious voice. "If this is what you really want."

"I do, but . . . I'm scared."

"There is no need to be afraid, Ana. This is meant to be. Tonight is the night of the Black Moon. It has to be tonight."

Chapter 5: Secrets

I awoke feeling as though my head was going to explode. As I looked around, I found I was back in my room and still fully clothed.

Thank God nothing happened, I thought as I recalled the events of last night. *How could I have allowed myself to become so vulnerable? And Adrian! Argh what a jerk! But . . . who was my saviour that night? If it wasn't for him, who knows what could have happened. It must have been Rogue. He must have come looking for me.*

As I got dressed in front of the mirror, I noticed my necklace was missing. Ink! He stole it from me. I raced down the stairs towards the kitchen in search of Rogue, but just as I was about to turn the doorknob, my hand froze, following the sounds of voices from within.

"Everything could have been ruined!"

"But it hasn't."

"Everything must happen according to plan! Nothing matters other than fulfilling the prophecy. Only then will the Lord reward us."

"The Lord's wishes shall be attained. You have my word. I'll see to Adrian later."

Curious as to who was inside, I opened the kitchen door to find Mr Rune and Vlad, who abruptly ceased talking the moment they saw me.

"Sophia! Ah, how are you feeling dear? I heard you had quite a fright last night," said Mr Rune, whose tone had completely changed from moments ago.

"Yeah . . . it wasn't the best night." I eyeballed them both at the same time.

"I am so sorry you had to go through that. Ink will be dealt with, you have my word. Don't worry about working for now. Take as much time off as you need, I expect you are recovering from the awful experience. Vlad and I need to pop out for some work, so we will see you later tonight."

"Mr Rune, sorry, but before you go, there were some questions I wanted to ask you. Things that . . . don't make any sense to me."

Vlad looked at Mr Rune, who gulped before answering. "Go on . . ."

"Ink mentioned some prophecy . . . something about me being the key. It doesn't make any sense."

Mr Rune looked as though he had been smacked in the face by a plank of wood. His skin suddenly looked paler. "That's because it's nonsense. Typical Incubus with his imagination running wild again and little filter over his mouth." Vlad chuckled as I watched his every move.

I had realised the Runes were clearly keeping secrets.

"He also seemed to know my mother, Ana," I continued. "Yet she never mentioned Ink before. He said . . . she needed help."

Surprisingly, confusion plastered across both of their faces at this piece of information.

"Did he . . . say what he helped her with by any chance?" asked Mr Rune with a raised brow.

"No. He never said." If only I had known what it was. The thought of Mother being in some kind of trouble pained me. I wasn't there to help her. My mind flickered back to the dreams I had been having. Wait . . . What if these dreams aren't really dreams? What if they're trying to tell me something? In that moment, I decided that I needed to stick around the Runes after all, until I found out what had happened with my mother.

The library was magnificent. It was a peculiar half-moon-shaped room with tall, chestnut bookshelves fixed across the walls. The flooring was the colour of rich ganache, with vibrant, leafy plants dotted around. An individual cylinder-shaped bookshelf stood alone, tall and proud in the centre of the room, as the light reflected off it through the pentagram-shaped glass ceiling. A small oak desk sat in front of it. I brushed my hand across some of the books, reading the titles as I went along. 'How to grow Potatoes'. 'First Degree in Astronomy'. 'Erotic Dreams'. 'How to Befriend a Dolphin.' The library clearly held an odd and wide variety of genres.

"I was wondering where you had gotten to," said a voice from the doorway, making my heart leap out of my chest.

"Rogue, you made me jump!" I gasped as he stood there laughing. "Actually, I'm glad you're here. I was actually looking for you earlier. I wanted to thank you for last night," I said, smiling at him.

"You're welcome," he said, returning the smile. "I'm sorry I left you. Vlad wasn't feeling too good, so I had to take him home, and I saw you were with Raven. But I came straight back looking for you." He stepped closer so that he was now facing me. "I'm glad you're ok. All I want is for you to be safe and happy. I really care about you, Sophia." He moved a strand of hair away from my face.

"I don't suppose you took back my necklace from Ink?" I blushed, abruptly changing the subject. "It's the only thing I have left of my parents."

"Erm, no, I didn't see a necklace. Sorry, Sophia. Are you sure he took it?" My heart sank hearing this.

"I'm sure because I watched him pull it off my neck," I narrated. "I also wanted to ask you about something. What prophecy was Ink talking about?"

"Prophecy? Ha, ha, there's no such thing. Your drink was spiked, Sophia, so it was probably the effects of the drug making you hallucinate," he explained as he scratched his head. His tone seemed slightly higher than normal, and his laughter appeared false.

He's lying. But why? He'd clearly heard Ink mention the prophecy, just as clearly as I had heard him say it, even in my drugged state.

"Yeah, I guess. Tell me, what did you do to Ink in the end? I mean, did you punish him in any way?"

"No. I simply threatened him to keep away from you and that he should never be seen talking to you again, which he agreed to."

"Oh . . . ok."

He's definitely lying, just like the others! Wait, if he wasn't the one who saved me last night, then who did?

I headed back to my room, the only place I felt safe. I had to come up with some sort of plan to find out what had happened to my mother, but if the Runes weren't going to talk, I had no idea how I was going to find out.

"Unless . . . What if Raven knows more?" I questioned myself.

As I walked into my room and closed the door shut, my heart dropped to the floor as I turned around to find Adrian lying on my bed, casually tossing an apple into the air and catching it with one hand. Flashbacks of the scene he'd created the night before came flooding back, making my blood boil and causing me to storm towards him.

"What the hell do you think you're doing?"

"Ever been to Hell? I could always send you there, if you like. Think you'd fit in nicely."

"Get out of my room, or I'll call Mr Rune!"

Adrian swung himself off the bed and wandered towards me slowly, and I began to brace myself. With each step he took, I took a step back, until I found myself pressed up against the wall. He stopped with his face inches away, his intense brown eyes burning into mine.

"No one else is here but you and me," he whispered.

Our eye contact never faltered. There was a moment of silence in which I felt time itself stop. I despised him, but I could not help feeling compelled towards him. There was this undeniable sexual energy that I couldn't ignore, making the hairs on my skin stand on end.

"I need you . . ." he began as my heart skipped a beat, "to pack your bags and leave." His tone turned serious.

"What? Why would I do that?"

"Because I want you gone. I don't want to see your face ever again. I can give you enough money to last you a lifetime. That shouldn't take much to convince you, I'm sure."

"I'm not going anywhere, Adrian. You can do whatever you want, I don't care. I'm not afraid of you."

Adrian pressed both of his hands firmly against the wall behind me, trapping me in the middle. "What if I decided to kiss those soft lips of yours? Would you care then?" His gaze drifted back and forth from my lips to my eyes.

My heart accelerated as my stomach filled with flutters. The temptation to grab him and taste his luscious lips was overwhelming, causing my knees to weaken. "I . . . I . . ." I stuttered, failing to find the words.

As quickly as he'd descended upon me, he stepped back. "I wouldn't kiss you. How could I kiss someone I despise so much?"

"I have no intention of being anywhere near you, either. You have yet to tell me why you hate me so much! I haven't done anything to you, and yet you choose to continue to be vile towards me. Why?"

"I don't have to explain anything to you, girl. Now, I'm not going to ask you again—"

"And my answer hasn't changed. I'm not going anywhere, Adrian Rune."

He glared at me for a moment before punching his fist through the wall behind me and storming out of the room.

I had only just realised how rapidly my heart was pounding. "Argh! What's wrong with you, Sophia? How could you desire someone so cruel to you?" I threw my hand against the wall behind me, hissing as I slapped the brick.

Feeling the need for some urgent fresh air, I headed outside. It was another beautiful, warm day with not a single cloud in sight. Birdsong echoed from the trees, whilst crystal droplets of water splashed back into the white marble fountain. As I walked the grounds, I soon found myself in front of one of the beautiful apple trees. Never had I seen apples look this ripe and shiny before. As my arm began to stretch out to pluck one of the ruby red apples, to my horror and disbelief, the branch suddenly began to grow and bend, taking the form of a serpent.

I shrieked and fell back onto the grass.

"Sssophia . . ." it hissed as it looked down at me.

"What are you doing on the ground, Sophia?" asked a voice from behind, making me scream.

I turned around to find Rogue looking at me. I swiftly spun my head back, analysing the tree, but there was no snake there. "Am I going mad?" I asked myself, not realising I had spoken out loud.

"Why would you think that?" Rogue lent me a hand, pulling me back up to my feet.

"Firstly, you need to stop creeping up on me like that," I said, catching my breath.

"Well, where's the fun in that? You look stressed. Is everything ok?" Lines appeared across his forehead.

I wanted to tell him the truth—heck, I wanted to be able to tell anyone the truth—but they would only think I was going crazy. I wasn't even too sure myself. "Yes . . . I'm fine thanks. Just, erm, just needed some fresh air," I lied as I glanced back at the tree.

"Well, try to get a good night's rest tonight at least."

"Oh, why is that?"

"Because it is a special day tomorrow." He smiled.

It was a special day. Tomorrow was the thirteenth of September: my birthday. I looked at him, wondering how he knew.

"Tomorrow is the night of the Black Moon, and we are throwing a party here at home to celebrate. I know you didn't have a great experience at the last party, but hopefully this one will make up for it."

My brows furrowed as I tried to recall where I had heard of the *Black Moon* before. "Black Moon? What is that?"

"Ever heard the story of the great goddess, Lilith?

"Lilith? As in the demon Lilith?"

"Yes. Legend has it that she is awakened every eve of the Black Moon, free to wander the earth for that one night. The Black Moon only occurs every five years," Rogue explained.

"So . . . why would you have a party in celebration of a demon?" I asked, looking puzzled.

"She's a mistakenly cursed soul. Mankind has filtered the truth so much that most of what remains are stories based on lies."

"Really? How exactly would you know that?"

"Trust me. I just know. The night is about exploring our deepest desires. I'm sure you must have some secret desires of your own," he said, throwing me a wink.

Although I knew Rogue was fond of me, images of Adrian appeared to fill my mind as quickly as I tried to block them out.

"Will Raven be coming to the party?" I asked, hastily changing the subject.

"Yes, she will be here. The party will begin at 8.30 pm."

"Great, looking forward to it!"

As Raven knew Ink well, there was a chance she may have more knowledge about how Ink knew my mother. Knowing that Raven and myself didn't see eye to eye, tomorrow was going to be a challenge. One that I had to win.

Chapter 6: The Black Moon

The new dawn brought forth rising emotions. It was the first birthday that I wouldn't get to celebrate with my mother since her plane had crashed. I never had the chance to meet my father, he passed away before I was born. Mother told me it was a shipwreck incident out at sea and they never recovered his body. The pit of my stomach was filled with emptiness. How greatly I desired to see them both, no one would fathom. I would give anything to be able to embrace them. Yet I knew that could never happen. I would never again hear my mother's voice, her laugh, her advice guiding me from right and wrong, or even being scolded by her. I would never again be able to sense her warmth, love and protection. It felt so unfair that they were snatched away by God before I could even say hello and goodbye.

As my emotions were all over the place, I found myself aimlessly wandering about the house, lost in my own thoughts. I ended up walking into a room that was clearly unused due to the amount of dust, cobwebs and drawn curtains.

All that was in the room was a large object covered by an old, stained fabric sheet. It sat on the oak flooring underneath a dusty, teardrop chandelier. I reached out to pull the sheet before pausing. I took a deep breath and, this time, yanked off the sheet. My eyes widened, and a smile stretched across my face. It was a beautiful, white grand piano.

Music had always been a love of mine, ever since my mother taught me how to play the piano and violin at the age of five. As I drew back the beige suede curtains, sunlight poured in, illuminating the entire room. Dust particles could be seen floating in each sunray. I brushed some of the dust off the satin stool with my hand before sitting down in front of the piano.

To my pleasant surprise, I opened the lid to find all the keys intact, and I gently brushed my fingertips across the keys before pressing a few.

It's still in tune, I thought smiling. *What should I play? I know. The song Mother used to sing to me every night.*

"Come now, child, dry your tears. For when you awake, you shall have no fears. Fire and Stone are in your soul. True love you will know, will make you whole." I paused for a moment, trying to catch my breath as my voice began to shake, my heart slowly crushing.

"Happy birthday . . . to me. Happy . . . birthday . . ." I sobbed, barely being able to speak.

Suddenly, I heard the door creak.

I spun around to see who was there, but there was no one. The door was ajar, but I was sure I had closed it behind me.

"This place is going to be the death of you, Sophia," I muttered to myself.

The evening drew in heaps of people, and I watched them filling the space in the large open hallway. Miniature moon-shaped lamps hung from the ceiling above, which was draped in a beautiful, black star cloth. Warm candles flickered in each corner of the room. The floor was covered in a bed of red rose petals, which guests carelessly walked over.

The attire for the night was black tie, so the men were fashioned in black fitted suits while the ladies wore long, elegant dresses.

Once again, I would have had nothing to wear, yet surprisingly, I was adorned in a gorgeous and elegant dress that evening. An hour before the party started, I had found a package left on my bed, neatly wrapped in black paper with a red net bow. Curious as to who had left it and what it could be, I ripped open the package to find a beautiful white gown. A note was left, simply containing three words: 'Happy Birthday, Sophia'. The backless dress hugged my waist as the remaining fabric fell to the floor. Black stones and white pearls embellished the top of the dress that curved around my chest. It was dazzling.

As I stood on top of the staircase leaning against the bannister, I watched and listened as the hallway quickly filled with the sounds of conversation, laughter and music. But all I cared about was finding Raven. My eyes searched the hall until, finally, they rested on a blonde-haired girl. She was wearing a red cocktail dress, and her hair was pinned in a neat bun that sat on the crown of her head. Her sapphire-blue eyes sparkled amongst the crowd. It was definitely Raven.

As I rushed to walk down the stairs, hoping I wouldn't lose sight of her, my heart sank as I tripped on the tail of my dress. I had lost control as my body tilted forward, ready to fall headfirst down the stairs. But in that split second, a firm hand grasped my right arm, holding my entire body weight in limbo. I was pulled back so quickly I found myself falling straight into their chest. The musky cologne oozing off of them seemed strangely familiar.

I looked up after catching my breath and, to my shock, saw the last person I expected to see.

Adrian didn't say a word but frowned, looking deep into my eyes, whilst still gripping my arm. I expected myself to feel angry at the fact that he'd dared even touch me, with just a slight appreciation for being saved; however, I felt something much stronger. The way he looked at me had sent ripples down my chest and back. My heart was pounding so deep and loud that all other noise seemed to be drowned by it. In that moment, I felt lost. I didn't even realise my left hand was resting on his chest.

As though Adrian had just realised he was still gripping my arm, he let go. "Watch where you're going, girl."

I wanted to thank him, but he didn't hesitate to hang around.

Being careful this time, I walked down the stairs whilst lifting up my dress. I didn't know if it was all in my head, but I felt people were, yet again, staring at me, making me vulnerable and uncomfortable.

Ignoring them, I looked out of the corner of my eye and spotted the hem of a red dress amongst the crowd. I sped towards her, but infuriatingly, it was as though with every step I took she had taken two steps away. I stopped chasing her, as, just then, the music was turned off and everyone began to form a ring, with Mr Rune walking into the centre.

He looked smart in his black tuxedo, his neat ponytail swaying as he moved.

"Ladies and gentlemen. Thank you all for coming on this glorious eve of the Black Moon. As you all know, it is our tradition to hold The Night of Desires every five years in her honour. For those who don't know, the Night of Desires consists of three elements. A dance, a challenge and a night alone. The first will be a dance. Dance and music were one of the greatest joys for our goddess of the night. To begin, you must first find yourself a partner you feel most attracted to. Choose wisely."

Following that, Mr Rune clapped his hands twice, and the ring dispersed as everyone began to couple up. Forgetting that I was also involved in the game, I continued to look around for Raven, until a voice behind me distracted my attention.

"Are you by any chance looking for me?" I turned around to see a dashingly handsome, blonde-haired man with a cheeky grin, and twinkling blue eyes. I opened my mouth to speak, but before I could say anything, he continued. "I must say, I am surprised you haven't been snatched up within seconds as someone's dancing partner."

"Oh, really? And why would that surprise you?"

"Come on, surely you must know how beautiful you are." He smiled, making my cheeks flush. I had never been any good at receiving compliments, mainly because I never really believed they were true. "Let me treat you like a princess tonight. Would you do me the honour of having this dance with me?" He was definitely a smooth talker.

Just then, I spotted Rogue approaching from between the crowd of people.

"Sophia, hey! You look amazing. Would you like to dance?" he asked, looking confident.

Truth be told, I didn't want to dance with either of them, let alone even be at this party, but I knew I had no choice but to play along. "Erm, sorry Rogue. This gentleman has just asked me first, so . . ." I watched as a wide smile stretched on the blonde man's face.

"Oh . . . that's ok. I'll find someone else to partner up with." He huffed, scowling at the blonde man before storming off.

The music was turned back on, and it appeared the dance was in the form of a waltz.

"I don't even know your name," I proclaimed, looking back at the blue-eyed man.

"The name's Michael," he said as he began to take my right hand while placing his other hand gently on my back.

I may enjoy the idea of dancing, but I was never any good at it myself. As we began to waltz around the hallway with my two left feet, making a right pig's ear of it all, I spotted Raven. One hundred needles pricked at my heart as I saw she was partnered up with Adrian. Envy began to flow through my veins, as much as I didn't want it to.

"You know, he isn't worth your time," said Michael after noticing me glance over at them several times.

"What? I don't know what you mean," I said, feeling slightly flustered and rather taken aback.

"You know exactly what I mean," he said with a cheeky smile. "Why want someone who doesn't make you feel as special as you are. He's just a miserable douchebag."

"He's different. Maybe the world needs more different," I shot back defensively, taking myself by surprise.

"The world is full of unique and mysterious things. You only need to open your eyes to see it," he whispered, throwing me a wink.

I looked at him for a moment as a slight smile began to edge across my face. Until I noticed Adrian looking over at us with, once again, a less than impressed looking Raven. His eyes were fixed in our direction.

The music abruptly stopped.

"Ladies and gentlemen. I hope you enjoyed the dance as much as I did," continued Mr Rune. "Now! We move on to the second element of the evening. Courage is something we all hope we possess, especially in times of need. Lilith possessed the courage to stand up to Adam after he refused to allow her to mount him, believing that her place remained beneath him. Lilith refused to accept this, as she wanted to be seen as equal, as God created both Adam and Lilith at the same time, which is why she decided to leave the Garden of Eden."

"Wait . . . Adam had more than one wife?" I whispered to Michael.

"Oh, how little you know, Sophia. Eve was Adam's second wife. Eve was created by God from the rib of Adam so that she would obey him, unlike the first. Lilith was

Adam's first wife. Adam was created from earth off the ground and Lilith was created from earth and dirt. People may worship God believing he is righteous, but he is the one responsible for the divide between men and women. He is the one who has created a world of discrimination. How Lilith was treated was unjust."

"What happened to her after she left the Garden of Eden?" I asked, but before he could answer, our attentions were drawn back to Mr Rune.

"This next part will be a challenge of courage. As you know, only one couple can proceed through to this stage. If you would all like to follow me outside." He led the way out.

The night sky appeared dark and dense as it concealed three quarters of the moon. A cylinder-shaped glass tank rested in the middle of the grounds, which appeared to be filled with water. Everyone gathered around the tank, forming yet again another ring.

"The task is fairly simple. A brave lady must enter this tank of water and stay afloat while their partner tries to rescue them. But there is, of course, a catch," confirmed Mr Rune. "The top border of the tank will be engulfed in flames, thus, making it much harder and dangerous to rescue your partner, yet not impossible. So! Without further ado, who volunteers to put themselves forward?"

Everyone remained silent. It appeared as though no one wanted to take the risk.

"We volunteer! It would be an honour," announced Michael as he gave me a little wink.

"What are you doing? I am not putting myself forward for this!"

"It's just a game, Sophia. One that I am confident I can win. No harm will come to you," Michael reassured.

"But it's risky! I mean, what if something went horribly wrong?"

"Nothing will go wrong."

"Aww, don't worry Sophia. We all understand if you're too afraid," Raven expressed in a patronising tone.

Adrian, who stood next to her, remained silent, but he appeared rather troubled.

"I am not *afraid* of anything, Raven," I shot back angrily.

"Then prove it," she said, smirking.

"All right, fine! Mr Rune, I accept the challenge and gladly volunteer myself," I proclaimed.

Michael smiled as I reluctantly took the hand he offered as he accompanied me towards the tank.

The whole thing seemed ridiculous to me.

Why can't they just play normal games, like chess?

"Sophia, dear, if you can begin by climbing up this ladder leaning against the tank and then slowly lower yourself in. The tank is only three quarters full, allowing you enough room to stay afloat and safe from the flames," explained Mr Rune.

I began to carefully climb the wooden ladder, lifting up the tail of my gown in one hand as I went along, which was about to be ruined. As I lowered myself in, I let out a gasp from the shock of the ice-cold water, which left me shivering.

Vlad walked up to the tank, holding a small matchbox. He took out a matchstick and, with a flick of his wrist, ignited a flame in the shape of a circle, covering the top border of the tank. I looked through the glass at Michael, who had a pondering look upon his face, clearly trying to figure out how he was going to get me out. The problem was that no one had anticipated the flames were going to rise as high as they were, not even Mr Rune from the reaction on his face.

However, all of that slipped my mind when I felt a slight tug at my ankle, making me jump. I looked down into the water, but there was nothing there. Only myself. Suddenly, as though by an invisible force, I was dragged under, taking in a large mouthful of water as I sank below.

It was as though a heavy weight latched onto my ankle, keeping me firmly at the base of the tank as I frantically tried to free myself from whatever it was. I could no longer see through the glass due to the disrupted water and the stinging, ice-cold sensation against my eyes.

With both hands on my ankle, I tried desperately to pull it towards me, but my attempts were futile. I could feel my lungs giving way as I desperately gasped for air, inhaling more water as I did so. Suddenly, I became still as every one of my muscles began to relax as the water consumed me as its prisoner.

This is the end, I thought as my eyes slowly shut.

Chapter 7: Worst Birthday Ever

I was in a small dimly lit room that contained nothing more than bare walls and a single wooden chair that was occupied. Mother appeared anxious as she tapped her fingers on the arms of the chair, as though she were waiting to be interviewed. I watched as she glanced at her watch several times. It was approaching eleven pm.

"This is ridiculous," she said out loud to herself. "What am I doing? I need to get home to Carlos before he begins to worry." She jumped to her feet and opened the door to leave, but she stopped, finding the same hooded figure she had spoken to in the dark alley looking back at her in the doorway.

"Where are you going, Ana?" he asked in a mundane voice.

"Home. This was a mistake, and, quite frankly, I am still perplexed as to how this all works. I have sat in this room for two hours now without the foggiest idea of what is happening."

"As I have promised, what you desire shall be yours tonight. Patience is a virtue, and all will be revealed soon."

"No. Something doesn't feel right. Thank you for wanting to help me, Aamon, and for your time, but I really ought to be getting home to Carlos."

"He is not at home, Ana." Her brows knitted together.

"What? No, of course he would be. It's very late. I'll just call him." She took out her mobile phone, and her hand shook as she dialled his number. Strangely, as soon as she called, a phone could be heard ringing from down the corridor. "That's strange, that's also Carlos's ringtone. Of course, it is just a coincidence," she assumed as she began to redial his number. Yet again, as soon as she began calling, a phone could be heard ringing from down the corridor.

Mother looked aghast as she stared at Aamon with wide eyes.

"As I said, Ana, he is not at home. He is here. But you can't see him, I'm afraid, at least not right now."

"Why? What are you doing with my husband?" she demanded.

Aamon remained silent.

"I am not going to be told by you or anyone else if I can or can't see my own husband!" She stormed passed Aamon. As she hurriedly walked left down the dark corridor of what *appeared to be an abandoned building, there seemed to be only one other door right at the end. She burst open the door, only to find a vacant office. However, there on the desk sat Father's phone. Mother spun around to face Aamon, who had followed behind her.*

"Please! Tell me where my husband is, Aamon, I beg you!"

"If you really want to know . . . he is outside. But know this. What is done cannot be undone. What is seen cannot be unseen."

Mother didn't take any notice of his words as she rushed out of the room towards the main exit of the old abandoned building.

I peeled open my eyes as I began to regain consciousness. I found myself looking up at the dark night sky as I felt the hard earth beneath me and heard low voices close by as my eyes wandered around.

"She will be fine, she is just unconscious for now," said Rogue.

"The Lord will not be pleased. He will be aware of this . . . You know nothing gets past him," confirmed Vlad.

"What I fail to understand is . . . how this is all possible? No one here possesses the ability. The only one who does is behind closed doors for now, where they are powerless," whispered Mr Rune.

"I, too, am at a loss for words. Even if someone here did possess the ability, they would be one of us, and would most likely be aware of the prophecy. If that is the case, why would they risk their lives trying to jeopardize what is meant to be?" asked Rogue.

After deciding I had heard enough, I began to sit up. Looking around, I saw the tank now lay in thousands of pieces as shards of glass glistened on the ground. An axe lay amongst the shattered glass. Someone had clearly smashed the tank to get me out. But who?

"Sophia, dear! You gave us all quite a fright. Are you all right?" Mr Rune rushed to help me to my feet.

"No. I'm not all right," I huffed, glaring at him. "But I would have been if it wasn't for this stupid challenge. Someone explain to me right now what the hell happened!" I ordered. My blood was boiling and my nostrils flared.

"What happened?" Michael appeared from behind. "Erm, Sophia . . . you drowned. You should have told me you were not a strong swimmer."

"I didn't *drown*, Michael. I was dragged down! By something . . . I mean, I couldn't see anything, but it was as though some invisible force was pulling me down," I explained, ignoring how crazy it all sounded.

"We didn't see anything else in the tank other than you, Sophia. What you are suggesting is some sort of supernatural presence, which is, quite frankly, absurd," chuckled Mr Rune.

"Is that right?" I eyeballed him.

Mr Rune winced as he stared back, as though he was analysing me.

As I couldn't trust them, I sure as hell was not intending on letting them know.

"Michael, my boy, please escort Miss Stone to her room so that she can rest," asked Mr Rune.

"That's ok, Mr Rune, I will take Sophia back," said a soft voice from behind.

As I turned to look, I was surprised to see that it was Raven. She was by herself, holding a thick, fluffy blanket in her arms that she began to unravel.

"Here, this should help keep you warm," she said, far from the usual tone she took with me.

"I'm fine, thanks," I uttered, returning a false smile which she had often given me.

"Please . . . let me help," she insisted.

I looked at her for a moment. She looked uneasy, and her eyes looked red and puffy, as though she had been crying. My frown softened before allowing her to drape the blanket around me. "Erm . . . thanks."

She smiled but seemed to avoid any eye contact. The house seemed unusually empty after coming back in from the eventful outdoors. "Are you . . . Are you ok?" asked Raven as we climbed the stairs.

"Could be better. At least I'm alive. Why do you even care anyway?"

"Listen, I'm so sorry. I should never have pressured you into doing that challenge. I was just jealous of you. I mean, look at you." I stared on at her with a raised brow. "I genuinely panicked when I thought you were. . . you know. I wouldn't have ever forgiven myself," she said, lowering her eyes. For the first time, her words sounded sincere, which made it easier to forgive her.

"I appreciate that. So, do you . . . Do you also believe I just *drowned*?"

"No," she spoke firmly. "You were staying afloat perfectly well, and I have no words to even begin to explain how it went wrong. It was shocking."

"Hmm. The Runes seem to think I just drowned," I said bitterly.

Raven rolled her eyes. "I have always thought that the Runes were odd, you know. Even Adrian isn't too keen, and that's his family."

Upon hearing Adrian's name, I realised I had not seen him since I regained consciousness. "Raven, where is Adrian?"

"He . . . erm, he went to his room early," she replied as I eyeballed her. "He wasn't feeling too well before the incident, I mean, so . . ."

"Why do I get the feeling you're lying?"

"I'm . . . I'm not—"

"Raven!"

"Ok, fine! But please don't tell him I told you. Sophia, it was Adrian who saved you. As soon as you were seen struggling underwater, he ran inside to find something that would help to break the tank. That's when he came back out with an axe. Think he hurt himself doing so too. I offered to help, but he refused."

How could this be? Why would the man who despises me most save my life? A hundred emotions danced through my mind, yet the most powerful felt as though a piece of my heart had been torn away at hearing Adrian was hurt.

"I need to see him."

"Erm, I don't know if that's wise. You know how he reacts around you. Do you really need that after everything you have been through tonight?"

"It doesn't matter. He can shout at me, belittle me, humiliate me, and even though I foresee it happening, it still won't hold me back from seeing him. He *saved* me Raven. . . And he's hurt."

"You know, I admit . . . I was jealous, not only of your beauty, but mostly because I could sense the electric energy whenever he looked at you. Something I could never have with him. But I understand why now. A man who looks at you the way he does could *never* hate you. Go. Go to him, Sophia." She smiled.

I smiled back and turned to leave, before pausing. "Oh, I almost forgot. I've been meaning to ask you something all night in fact, I just—" I started before she cut me off.

"Listen, don't worry about asking me anything right now. Go to him. I'll come and see you tomorrow," she said, waving me away.

As I made my way towards Adrian's room, lost in my own thoughts, I had no idea what to expect upon entering. My last visit to his room was horrid. But this time . . . I wasn't afraid. This time was different. All I knew in that moment was how much I wanted to see him. As I turned the brass doorknob, I slowly pushed open the door. The room was dark and only dimly lit by a small bedside lamp.

Adrian was propped up on his bed, shirtless.

My eyes rested on his upper right arm, which was oozing with blood, yet he didn't seem to be bothered by it. In fact, he appeared in a daze. As I stepped closer towards him, he looked up, startled to see me.

"You know, for someone who hates me so much, you sure do a good job in keeping me alive. Wouldn't it be easier for you if you just allowed me to die? Instead, you saved my life twice in one night. Why?"

"Don't flatter yourself. I would have done it for anyone. But I didn't want anybody's dirty blood spilt on our property. Especially yours. I told you to leave, but you chose not to listen."

"If you tell me again, I'm afraid my decision to stay still remains strong. More than ever now," I said softly.

He watched as I began to move closer towards him. My heart was pounding deeply, as it always seemed to do whenever I was in his presence.

"Even after everything that has happened, you are either very brave or very stupid to have come back into my room in the middle of the night. I'm leaning more towards the latter."

I didn't respond, just continued to look at him in silence. His empty words no longer seemed to frighten me.

"Get out of my room before you regret coming here. If you're not going to leave this place, then at least keep out of my sight," he said in a raised voice

But I continued to remain silent as I gazed deep into his eyes, aware of my heart pounding away in my chest. I wasn't going to walk away. Not tonight. Reaching for the bottom of my soaked dress, I began to slowly pull it up. Confusion was plastered all over Adrian's face as he continued to watch in silence. I proceeded to tear off a large strip of the fabric, destroying what remained of my beautiful gown. Moving closer towards Adrian until I was inches away from his face, I sat on the bed beside him and began to wrap the fabric tightly around his open wound.

Adrian remained silent as he watched me carefully bandage his arm. Once I had finished securing the fabric tightly in a knot, I looked back at him to find him looking at me in awe. For a moment, we gazed deep into one another's eyes, as though we were looking through windows into our souls. My gaze lowered and slowly fell to his lips. As much as I wanted to kiss those soft lips of his, I wanted to know that he felt the same.

"Thank you for saving me, Adrian." I smiled. As I stood up and turned to leave, he grabbed my wrist, stopping me in my tracks.

I knew it! I knew he felt the same way about me!

"Don't go falling for me, Sophia. You'll only get hurt. You and I are not meant to be," he whispered behind me. A thousand knives pierced my heart upon hearing his words. I remained silent, and, without looking back at him, I continued to leave the room.

Back in my room, I threw myself onto the bed and buried my head into my soft silk pillow as tears began to pour down my face. Even without any lights on, the room seemed darker than usual, but in that moment, the darkness seemed comforting. My heart felt as though it were made of shattered glass. I had never experienced such strong feelings for someone the way I did for Adrian. But he didn't want me back. How was this even a shock?

I hate him. He's an ass.

It really was the worst birthday ever. As my emotions soared, I continued to sob into my pillow.

"Come now, child, dry your tears. For when you awake, you shall have no fears . . ." echoed a gentle voice.

My heart leapt from my chest as I jolted upright and tried to scan the room within the darkness. "It's just in your head, Sophia. Whatever you're thinking right now is impossible," I reassured myself out loud.

"Fire and Stone are in your soul . . ." the voice continued.

My eyes darted towards the window sill. A faint outline of a woman could be made out sitting on the windowpane. Terror and hope struck me at the same time as my heart somersaulted in my chest.

"True love you will know, will make you whole," she finished.

"Mother?" Adrenaline flowed through me.

There was no response and no movement.

I plucked up the courage to pull myself out of bed and tiptoe towards the figure. But as I edged closer, I heard something that made my spine crawl.

"Sssophia."

As soon as I heard it, the figure vanished as quickly as it had appeared, leaving me feeling both frightened and disappointed. As I ran to turn all the lights on, I searched the room, but there was no one else there.

Was it really my mother, or just a figment of my imagination?

I didn't have the answers to the questions swimming through my mind. All I knew was that only my mother and I knew that song.

Chapter 8: The Charm

After a restless night, I was awoken the next morning by a double knock on the door. Not feeling my normal energetic self, I shuffled myself off the bed and dragged my feet towards the door, which I opened to find Uriel looking back at me.

"Miss Stone, you have a visitor waiting for you outside. Your friend, Raven Belltree," he confirmed, before he proceeded to skulk away.

The weather had turned bitter that morning as grey clouds clustered. I could tell a storm was brewing.

Raven was sat on the edge of the marble water fountain dressed in a black turtleneck jumper and blue jeans. She smiled as she spotted me approaching. "I told you I would come see you today."

I perched beside her, wishing I had worn something cosier.

"So . . . how was last night with Adrian?"

"He's not interested. I know that much," I muttered.

"That is so far from the truth, you have no idea. He is crazy about you, Sophia. He's never shared his feelings towards you with me, but it's just obvious. I see the way he looks at you."

"His words suggest otherwise."

"But—"

"Anyway, if it's all right with you, I would rather not talk about him," I said, cutting her off. "I actually wanted to talk to you about something important. My mother and . . . some sort of prophecy. You're friends with Ink. Did he ever talk to you about a prophecy?"

"Prophecy? You mean like one of those things that foretell the future? I thought those were only in fiction books."

"Listen. A lot of strange things have been happening ever since I moved here." I then began to explain all that had happened since living with the Runes as she watched me in bewilderment.

"Wow . . . It all sounds almost unbelievable. I mean, I knew the Runes were odd, but I never realised they were this odd," Raven expressed. "First of all, Ink and I aren't close friends. He's more of an acquaintance. So, I'm afraid I have never heard him mention your mother before, and I am unsure as to how he would have even known her. I'm sorry, Sophia, I wish he had mentioned Ana to me so I could help you." Her words and eyes were sympathetic. My heart filled with disappointment. "As for the prophecy, though, I did overhear Rogue briefly discussing it with Mr Rune one evening, a week before you moved here. I couldn't make out everything they were saying. Something about it being kept well hidden. But when I asked Rogue about it, he made out that I had misheard what was said, as though I had just imagined it."

"Yeah, well, lying seems to be a habit of theirs, which is why I need to uncover the truth. I'm just not sure how. I know the prophecy has something to do with me. But these dreams must mean something, too."

"Wait a minute!" Raven's eyes lit up and a smile appeared on her face. "Maybe we can find some answers in the library. There must be some book that gives us more information about the Black Moon. You said Aamon in your dream mentioned the Black Moon to your mother and that she was in that abandoned building on that exact night. So, if we try to understand more about the Black Moon, maybe that will bring us one step closer to figuring out what's going on."

"You know, don't let anyone ever tell you you're just a pretty face," I smiled cheekily. It sounded like a good plan, especially seeing as we didn't have any others.

We made our way towards the library through the eerie silence of the mansion.

"Woah . . . I have never been to this part of the house before. This is something," Raven gasped.

"It really is." I glanced around, as though I were also seeing it all for the first time.

Without further ado, we split and scanned the bookshelves in search of something that would help us, coming across more peculiar titles as we did so.

A quiet, pleasant meow echoed through the room, distracting our attention. We looked around to find a small black kitten perched on the floor on the other side of the cylinder bookshelf, looking up at us with its big azure eyes.

He was adorable.

"Hello. How did you manage to find your way in here?" Raven asked as she picked up the kitten and began stroking him.

"Looks like you may have found yourself a new friend," I said, smiling. Although I found it strange as to how a kitten had found its way in, there were stranger things to worry about.

"Oh no, I can't keep him. My father's allergic to cats. But you can keep him!"

"What? No, I can't . . ."

"Why not? How can you say no to these big blue eyes of his?" she asked, holding the kitten in front of her face.

He licked her cheek, almost as though he were thanking her.

"Because I feel it's wise not to get attached to anyone or anything. Anyone I seem to get close to only ever ends up leaving me," I muttered.

Almost as though the kitten could understand me, he leapt out of Raven's grip and rested both its front paws on my leg, purring as he looked up at me. I couldn't deny how heart-warming it felt.

"Aww see. How could you not love something as cute as that?"

I picked up the kitten and cradled him in my arms. "Well . . . I guess it would be nice. Looks like you're stuck with me. I think I'll call you . . . Taboo."

Taboo gave a pleasant meow as though he approved.

As our search continued, Raven managed to land her hands on one particular book: 'Mythology of Astronomy'. "There's a page in here about the Black Moon and Lilith," Raven reported. "To be honest, there isn't much written in here that we don't know already, except for this. Listen here:

"After Lilith left the Garden of Eden, she took full advantage of her freedom and self-empowerment and indulged in lustful, sinful pleasures with many demons, as they each fulfilled her sexual desires. From this, she bore many babies. However, God decided to curse Lilith for this. Every child she bore with another demon would only live a short life. As a result, none of Lilith's children ever saw past the age of one."

She looked up at me. "You mentioned that in your dream something was going to happen on the night of the Black Moon . . ."

"So?"

"So . . . if your mother, Ana, was infertile and, as Lilith couldn't have children of her own, maybe she helped Ana by fixing her infertility. I mean, she is a goddess, and who would understand more than her."

"That is the most ridiculous thing you have ever said," I uttered, rolling my eyes.

"Is it really, though, Sophia? I know it sounds crazy, but these *dreams* are clearly not just dreams. More like visions of the past. Which means Ana was infertile, yet here you stand. Explain that."

"I . . . I can't." As ridiculous as it sounded, it was still the only explanation we had so far. "This is hopeless." I crossed my arms over my chest in a huff.

"Let's go out for drinks," said Raven.

"What?"

"Listen, I think we deserve a break. You especially. We've been at this for hours. We'll find more answers, trust me. But first, drinks!"

The evening came around quickly, bringing along dark clouds and strong winds. Raven had gone back home, and we were to meet this evening at The Charm.

After throwing on a pair of fitted jeans and a cosy woolly jumper, I made my way outside, expecting to find Uriel waiting in the Rolls Royce. But neither the car nor Uriel were anywhere to be seen. In its place, however, stood a magnificent black Harley-Davidson, which, to my dismay, was being revved by Adrian whilst he sat on the bike wearing black ripped jeans and a black leather jacket.

I soon found myself reluctantly walking towards him. "Ahem," I coughed to get his attention over all the racket he was making.

He glanced at me casually.

"Have you seen Uriel? He was supposed to be taking me to The Charm this evening."

"He had to take the Rolls to a garage for some repair work. So instead, it's your lucky day. I will be taking you to The Charm." He grinned.

This is the last thing I need right now, I thought on a groan.

"Don't waste your precious time on me, I'll make my own way down."

"Oh really? And how were you planning on doing that exactly?"

"I'll catch a taxi."

"In which case, you will be waiting around forever for one. Taxi's don't come to this part of the town," he explained.

I was beginning to run out of excuses, but just then, a bright red Porsche arrived through the black iron gates and drove up towards us. "Who is that?"

"Michael," muttered Adrian, who watched on unimpressed.

Michael exited the vehicle wearing a maroon fitted shirt and black jeans, looking rather smart. "Must have missed the invite by the looks of it," he smiled as he looked at us both.

"Michael, what are you doing here?" I asked curiously.

"Well, I was actually coming to see you. I still feel ashamed about what happened that night with the challenge, and I wanted to make it up to you. I was wondering if you wanted to go out tonight somewhere. Just the two of us," he added as he glanced back at Adrian, who looked annoyed.

"Oh wow, erm . . . I was actually kind of on my way out already to meet Raven at The Charm."

"Oh, that's ok. Well, hey, let me at least give you a ride there."

"No need to inconvenience yourself, Michael, I can take her," Adrian cut in.

You could tell neither of them liked each other; you could cut the tension with a knife.

"Well, I am sure Sophia will feel much warmer inside my Porsche," said Michael.

"But she will arrive much quicker if she rides with me," Adrian shot back.

I found it rather peculiar watching them both bicker over who was going to take me.

"I tell you what. How about we let Sophia decide who she wants to go with, hey?" Michael said, both of their gazes now fell on me.

My heart wanted me to go with Adrian. Nothing would make me happier. But that would only be a good idea in a world where he wanted me as much as I wanted him. Knowing that he didn't feel the same about me, there was no need to put myself in that situation again.

"I choose Michael," I confirmed.

Michael looked positively beaming.

"Sophia, I wanted to talk to you," said Adrian, which took me by surprise.

"I don't have anything to say to you, Adrian."

"You're really going to get in a car with the person who was so sure he could save you?"

"Why do you even care? I am not your responsibility, Adrian. I am free to make my own choices . . . and my own mistakes," I said through gritted teeth.

Adrian didn't respond, but he looked at me with furrowed brows.

"Sophia, come. We had better get you to The Charm, or Raven will start wondering where you have gotten to." Michael held open the passenger door like a gentleman.

I paused as I glanced back at Adrian. My heart ached and cried out for him. I wanted to be with him, and I could have easily chosen to ride with him, but I couldn't allow my attachment to grow anymore. It was time to move on.

"Well, that was awkward. You look beautiful today, by the way," said Michael as he drove towards The Charm. "Not that you don't look beautiful every day, I mean," he chuckled nervously.

"Thanks." A smile half etched across my face "So, erm, tell me more about yourself," I asked in an attempt to change the subject.

"Ask me anything you want to know, and I'll tell you."

"All right. Erm, do you live with your parents or by yourself?"

"With my parents currently. I'm an only child, which is why they always suffocate me so much. Sometimes I wish they would just disappear," he huffed.

"No longer having your parents is something I wouldn't wish upon anyone. You are lucky to have them. Others are less fortunate," I muttered, lowering my gaze.

"Right yes . . . Sorry, I didn't mean—"

"It's fine, don't worry about it."

The atmosphere had quickly turned awkward.

Luckily, it didn't take us long to arrive at The Charm. The place was true to its name. From the outside, it appeared to be a slightly wonky-shaped cottage that rested in front of a wooded area. Two tall, strong trees stood proudly on either side of the cottage as miniature candlelit lanterns hung off each branch.

As I stepped through the oak doorway, I looked around. A row of beautiful blossom trees stood in the centre of the room, paving a walkway to the back, where the bar was located. Tables shaped like large tree trunks were situated on the left and right side of the room. The theme of hanging lanterns continued as they hung from the wooden beams on the ceiling.

I spotted Raven, who was waving at us from the far-right hand corner.

"Took you long enough! Oh, good, you brought an extra drinking partner. Will you be joining us, Michael?"

"I'd love to join." He smiled as we both sat down.

"Welcome to The Charm. What can I get you all today?" asked a high-pitched voice. A small, chubby waitress stood beside our table. She had curly red hair and overly large, round spectacles propped on the end of her long nose. She smiled at us, showing a sct of overly large two front teeth as she looked at us through her beady eyes.

"We will have three gnomes please," said Raven as I looked at her puzzled.

"Make that four," said a familiar voice from behind me, making my heart skip a beat.

I turned my head to find Adrian standing there.

"Adrian, what are you doing here?" asked Raven.

"Yeah, don't you have somewhere else to be? Anywhere but here," fired Michael, who looked utterly displeased at his arrival.

"Nowhere else I'd rather be, *Michael*." Adrian grinned. His gaze slowly turned to me, giving me a fluttery feeling before I quickly looked elsewhere. "Besides, I could ask you the same thing. Didn't think you enjoyed spending time intruding on a girls' night out."

"You can talk. Are you not doing the exact same thing?"

"Raven invited me," announced Adrian.

I looked at Raven, who seemed confused, but her expression soon changed quickly.

"Oh yes, of course I did, silly me. Ha, ha."

I glared at her, recognising her all too familiar fake laugh.

Adrian sat opposite me.

The atmosphere became more intense as I watched Michael and Adrian, who were now gawping at one another.

The silence was suddenly broken by the same high-pitched voice as the waitress returned with our drinks, which came in mugs shaped like gnomes.

"I know, let's play a game. Think it might break the ice here a bit," said Michael. "It's called Guilty as Charged. We all go around one by one, each making a statement that can be either true or false. If anyone is actually guilty of doing the deed, including the player who said it, then you must drink! A great simple way to get trolleyed! I'll start."

"Seems a fitting idea for someone who enjoys playing games himself," Adrian threw in, but Michael ignored him.

"I am guilty of missing a curfew."

"Really?" asked Adrian, looking bemused.

"Just play the bloody game," Michael snapped back.

All four of us took a large swig of our drinks, which, to my pleasant surprise, tasted like skittles.

Next was Raven's turn. "I have a great one. I am guilty of . . . falling in love."

I felt a prick in my heart as my eyes darted from Adrian to the floor. I was contemplating lying and not drinking, but then I saw that Adrian had taken quite a few gulps of his before resting his glass back down on the table, staring at it as he did so. A wave of jealousy struck, causing me to drink my glass almost dry. *Who did he love? How is he even capable of such a thing?*

Both Michael and Raven hadn't drank.

It was my turn next, and I was eager and intrigued to find out more about Adrian.

"Erm, I am guilty of kissing someone." I regretted it as soon as the words escaped my lips. I had wasted my turn as, of course, Adrian would drink. I had seen him in bed with other women. I also realised only too late that my question would backfire on myself after I noticing I was the only one who did not drink.

"You've never been kissed before?" Michael asked, wide-mouthed.

"No . . . I haven't," I admitted, fixing my gaze on my drink.

"That's because she's a virgin," chuckled Raven.

"Raven!" I shouted as my cheeks turned crimson.

"Are you?" asked Adrian.

I looked at him and saw the familiar look of admiration. "Yeah," I muttered, feeling embarrassed.

I was half expecting him to make a mockery of all this, but he didn't say anymore and instead continued to take his turn. "I am guilty . . . of hiding my true feelings from someone," Adrian stated.

I watched Raven and Michael sip their drinks . . . including Adrian. I found myself hesitating and felt almost vulnerable. "I need to go to the bathroom," I lied, excusing myself as swiftly as possible to walk away from a very awkward situation.

Annoyingly, Raven had also decided to follow.

As I went through the back door and pushed opened the bathroom door, I let out a muffled scream as a large empty sack was thrown over me, trapping me inside. I was lifted and thrown over the back of their shoulder before they proceeded to take me out through the fire exit.

"Oi, let her go, you big oaf!" I heard Raven shout.

The sound of a loud thump was heard, followed by silence, after which the stranger continued to take me outside against my will as I wriggled around inside the bag, screaming as much as I could. I couldn't scream for long, however, as I was thrown into the back of a vehicle, banging my head hard off the side as I did so, and then once again, everything became dark and my muscles began to relax.

Chapter 9: Holuny Woods

wo figures could be seen wandering through the trees.

"How much farther?" Mother asked Aamon in her frustrated state as they both trekked through the dark woods.

Aamon remained silent.

"Where are we?"

"Holuny Woods," he replied. "This is where Carlos will be."

Suddenly, a faint amber glow could be seen emerging from the distance, and the closer they got, the more prominent the glow became.

"Is that . . . something burning?" Mother asked, looking terrified.

Again, Aamon remained silent.

Finally, they had reached the mouth of Holuny Woods, and what appeared to be a glow of light turned out to be a frightfully large burning ring of fire. The ring was almost five feet tall and created from stacked wood.

Thinking that she might have seen someone within the burning ring, she took a deep breath before edging forwards to see.

I peeled open my eyes to find that my wrists and ankles had been tied to a tree trunk, which appeared to be at the opening of a wooded area beginning to darken. I searched the open land in front of me through the pouring rain to find no one and nothing but an empty red truck. Panicking as realisation kicked in, I fought to escape the bindings. I pulled, kicked, tugged, and screamed until my wrist burned raw and my ankles screamed louder than me.

"Ssophia . . . home . . . Come home."

The familiar hissing voice made my muscles seize as the hairs on my arms stood on end. I wanted so much to put a face to the voice so I knew I wasn't going mad, but there was no one there. Just then, the sound of twigs and branches being trodden on by someone behind me echoed.

"Who's there?"

Only silence responded for a moment.

"Hello love," said a deep voice in my ear, making my heart leap from my chest.

A figure leered from the woods behind me. He was a tall, bald and stocky looking man, with a tattoo on the back of his neck, which read, *Bellator Luminis*.

"Who . . . who are you?" I tried to catch my breath in my petrified state. "What do you want from me? Why have you brought me here?"

"So many questions . . . so little time . . . for you. My name is Lux. I'm not here to beat around the bush. I have brought you here to end your life."

"You want to kill me . . . but why?" My heart raced, my palms began to sweat with fear, yet my blood also boiled with rage.

"Because killing you means destroying the only chance of unlocking the gates and preventing damnation on Earth. Killing you now would be saving your soul."

"Gates? Soul? You're not making any sense, you're just . . . talking in riddles!"

"Life in itself is a riddle, do you not think?" Lux asked.

"Why here? Why bring me here to kill me out of all places?" I asked, ignoring his question.

"It has to end where it all began. There is no point explaining anymore. The task must be completed. I will make this swift for you, Sophia. It will all be over before you know it." He raised his left hand, clutching a gun.

My muscles had seized from terror. I had lost the power to scream.

This is the end.

But just as the thought crossed my mind, Lux let out a yelp as a large rock flew from behind me, smashing against Lux's head and causing the gun to drop out of his grasp.

I turned my head as much as I could to see three figures running towards us from between the trees, filling my insides with relief. Lux tried to pick up the gun but received a nasty surprise in doing so, as Taboo, who came leaping from the trees, sunk his teeth into Lux's hand, making him cry out in pain. Lux's face came into contact with Adrian's fist, whilst Michael held Lux's arms back as much as he could.

"Oh my God, Sophia! Are you all right?" asked Raven, who came running over and hurriedly untied the ropes around my wrists and ankles.

"Raven, I'm fine. I'm so glad you all found me. A few more seconds later . . . I don't think I would be here thanking you. How did Taboo get here?" I asked after hearing him meow.

"He must have gotten into the back of Michael's car before you left the mansion." Raven had now managed to untie the ropes, setting me free.

Our attentions turned to the bloody fight happening in front of us with Lux, Adrian and Michael. Lux, unfortunately, had managed to escape from Michael's grasp and threw a forceful blow at Michael, which completely knocked him out.

"Michael!" shrieked Raven, who appeared upset. "Erm, and Adrian! Be careful," she quickly added, becoming aware of her reaction towards Michael and catching me glance at her with a raised brow.

I turned back just in time to watch as Lux pulled out a sharp, silver blade from inside his jacket, and my heart stopped. "Adrian, look out!"

Lux tried to stab Adrian twice in swift movements, but Adrian's reaction was, thankfully, too quick. Adrian managed to swing himself over Lux, snatching the blade from his grip as he did so, and pulled Lux's head back into an armlock with the blade resting on his throat.

In that moment, I wanted Lux to suffer. I wanted him to feel pain. I wanted him to die a slow death.

"Who sent you? Tell me now, or I will slit your throat slowly," Adrian demanded.

"Ha, ha, we both know you are going to kill me either way. I have tried to do the girl a favour by protecting her from a worse life. You think you're a hero by protecting the girl from me. It's your kind she needs protecting from," he grimaced.

"Her name . . . is Sophia," said Adrian, and with that, he sliced Lux's throat in a slow, blood-stained slash.

Blood sprayed from the wound like a garden sprinkler before he collapsed lifelessly to the ground.

Raven and I ran towards Adrian and Michael, who still lay unconscious.

"Is he going to be all right?" I asked.

"He will be fine," said Adrian.

"Who was he?" I asked.

"Bellator Luminis. It's Latin for Warrior of Light. There must be more of them."

"Let's hope not. I'll take Michael back with me in his car and get him in some warm clothes," said Raven. "I mean, I don't want him to catch a cold," she quickly added after seeing me grin.

"Bring him back to the mansion, you can both rest there. I'll take Sophia back with me," said Adrian.

I didn't say anything. I knew I was safe now with him.

After Adrian helped lift Michael into the car, we both watched in silence as the Porsche drove away. Adrian quietly walked over to his bike and mounted it, then looked over at me, and I realised I was still stood in the same spot.

My mother was looking for my father here in Holuny Woods in my dream. Could this be the exact same place?

I walked towards Adrian quietly and mounted the bike behind him.

"You should hold on tight," he said softly.

A wave of adrenaline rushed through me as my heart beat faster and I wrapped my arms around his strong waist.

Chapter 10: A Night to Remember

The wind and rain felt strangely calming against my skin as we rode back to the mansion. Even with the miserable weather and my near-death experience, I was surprisingly happy just being in Adrian's presence. It took no time at all to arrive at the mansion, I just wished the journey could have been longer.

We finally came to a halt, and I noticed the Porsche was also parked up. I stepped off the bike and stood in front of Adrian, looking up at him.

"You risked your life for me today," I said.

"I would do it again."

I looked on at him with knitted brows, taken aback by his response. "But . . . I thought—"

"I would be lying if I said I didn't feel suffocated whenever you are not around. If I said that my heart doesn't burn whenever I look into your eyes. If I said I didn't think you are so precious that I would spend the rest of my life protecting you," he confessed, gazing deep into my soul.

An electric wave of affection rippled down my spine.

"I've tried to hate you, to push you away. But the more I did, the more I became compelled towards you."

"Then . . . why lie?"

"Because I wasn't lying when I said we can never be together."

"Why?"

"Because I'm not good for you, which is why I tried to make you leave before. You're not safe if you're with me."

I moved closer to Adrian without faltering our eye contact and gently placed my hand on his face, gaining his full attention.

"You have proved to me time and time again that I am safe wherever you are. The moment I stopped fearing you, Adrian, was the moment I realised how much I wanted you. I believe you have a bigger heart than you think."

"Sophia, listen to me! Neither one of us can have what we want from this. This path can only lead to heartache if we are together."

"Then I am prepared to walk that path for eternity if that's what it means to be with you."

There was a moment of silence. The powerful aura we were giving off was undeniable. I watched as his gaze fell to my lips, which was inches from his. All I could think about in that moment was how much I wanted to kiss him.

"Sophia? Adrian? What are you doing out in the rain? You will catch a cold. Come inside," said Mr Rune, startling us both.

We walked inside the dry and warm mansion, and I watched as Mr Rune shut the door behind us. I didn't realise how late it was until I glanced over at the grandfather clock, where both hands were pointing to twelve.

"Is everything all right? Did you have a good night?" asked Mr Rune, glancing from Adrian to me

"Yes, thank you. It was a great evening," I lied. I didn't trust Mr Rune, and I couldn't be sure he didn't send Lux himself to kill me. I wondered if he was disappointed to see me alive.

"Good. I'm glad. Well, Raven and Michael are upstairs. She said Michael had drunk a lot and fallen over, hence the bruising on his forehead, so Uriel has made a room up for him."

I was so glad to hear Raven also didn't say anything to Mr Rune.

"I'll just go and see how he is before I go to bed. Goodnight, Mr Rune." I smiled, looking directly into his eyes, as though I could see right through him.

He returned a slightly crooked smile and nodded.

"I'll follow you," said Adrian.

Michael's room was around the corner from mine. As we entered, I was glad to see that Michael was conscious again and smiling as he sat up in bed.

Raven perched on the edge of the bed next to him.

"I don't know about you guys, but after tonight, I think I'm ready to go out there and start fighting crime," Michael chuckled.

"Michael . . . about tonight and, erm, helping me . . . Just wanted to say . . ." said Adrian, who seemed to be finding it hard to say what he wanted.

"No need to thank me. I've got your back," said Michael, winking.

Adrian grinned.

"Sophia, did you want me to sleep in your room tonight?" asked Raven.

"Don't go," said Michael to Raven. "I mean, erm, it would be nice if you could stay tonight. You know, just in case I pass out again or something," he added, trying to play it cool.

I couldn't help but smile.

"We will leave you both to get some rest. See you in the morning," said Adrian as we left the room. He turned to look at me. "I guess this is goodnight then."

"It doesn't have to be," I whispered.

He hesitated for a moment.

I could hear the drumming of our hearts in the silence.

Without another word, he walked away towards his room, leaving me alone.

I shut the door behind me after entering my room and leaned against it. *How could life be so cruel?* I had finally found my happiness, but it was slipping through my fingertips like water. My heart was bleeding because I realised, for the first time, that I had fallen in love. The more he pushed me away, the more I loved him.

As I began to walk towards my bed, the door opened and shut behind me. To my pleasant surprise, I turned to find Adrian in my room.

"I thought it would be simple . . . to just walk away. But I don't want to exist in a world without you with me," he said softly. He lifted my face with his hand as he gazed back into my eyes. "I would burn for you if it meant protecting you, Sophia."

"But I would burn *with* you," I whispered.

He lowered his gaze once again to my lips and, with confidence, pressed his lips firmly against mine.

He didn't light a flame in my heart. He lit a wildfire. I had surrendered myself completely as I leaned into him, my fingers running through the back of his hair.

He lifted me up onto the bed, and I felt the weight of his body pressed against mine as his lips caressed my neck. Within moments, our clothes had come off. The touch of his tongue gliding slowly up my thigh, teasing me, drove me insane.

Spreading my legs apart and wrapping them around his torso, he slowly pushed himself deep inside me as we both let out a gasp. His hips began thrusting between my legs, both of us in a pool of sweat. My nails ran up his back, and I held on to his broad shoulders as he kissed me hard. Feeling how excited I was only made him thrust harder and faster. My senses were heightened as a heated pulse spread between my legs. All I knew in that moment was how much I wanted him. I wanted all of him. As though someone new had awoken inside me, I swung myself on top of Adrian.

He smiled before letting out a moan as I lowered myself on top of him. He felt too good. The air was thick with ecstasy. My hips moved back and forth rapidly, and the pleasure became so intense that, suddenly, the most magical thing happened. Through our panting, an intense, sensual wave rippled through my entire body as we both climaxed simultaneously.

I collapsed on top of him, kissing him gently on the lips before laying in his arms.

"I love you, Sophia," he whispered.

"I love you, too," I confessed.

Chapter 11: Secrets Revealed

Was it all a dream? Just one big, beautiful dream? I could sense the glow of the morning light through my eyelids. I wanted to open my eyes, but I was too afraid. Afraid that it had all just been a dream and that Adrian was never mine.

I slowly opened my eyes and felt a sudden pang of heartache. Adrian was nowhere to be seen. I sat up in bed, scanning the room to find no one but myself . . . all alone. It couldn't have been a dream. It was all too real. *But what if . . . he used me and then . . . abandoned me?* My heart pounded. I didn't know what to think.

However, my fears soon melted away as Adrian walked into the room, along with Taboo, who ended up climbing onto my bed before resting.

I was drowned with such utter relief that I couldn't hide the huge smile on my face.

He was holding a small black box. "Did you think I had left you?"

"No," I lied, trying to keep my cool.

He simply smiled as though he saw right through me. He had such a beautiful smile. "I went back to my room to get you something. I decided it would look better on you than me." He passed me the small black box.

With no idea what was inside, I pulled the lid off the box, and, to my complete joyful surprise, my silver locket shined back at me.

"Oh, Adrian! I thought I had lost this forever! Where did you—?"

"It was me who brought you home the night of Ink's party. I made sure I snatched it out of his slimy grasp before he ran off. I was going to give it to you earlier, but I never knew when the moment was going to be right. Until now."

I leaned in close to Adrian and kissed his soft lips. "Thank you, Adrian. This means a lot to me. Can I ask you something?"

"Anything," he said.

"I remember Ink mentioned a prophecy that night you saved me. He also said that I was the key and he also knew my mother . . . What does it all mean?"

The moment of truth.

There was a minute of complete silence as Adrian had become rather still.

"Adrian?"

"Promise me something," he asked in a serious tone.

"Anything."

"What I'm about to tell you . . . maybe hard . . . to believe. After I tell you, you won't want to be with me anymore, and I wouldn't blame you. Just promise me, after you leave, you'll continue to live your life and be happy."

"Adrian, you're worrying me. Please, just tell me. Whatever it is, we will get through it together."

"I'm . . . I'm not human," he said.

I blinked a few times and continued to look on at him in silence.

"Dimitri, Vlad, Rogue . . . even Michael. We are related, but not in the way you think. We are . . . Angels . . . Fallen Angels."

The room became so silent that you would be able to hear a pin drop on the floor.

I continued to look at him blankly.

"There are many like us, both Old Stars and New. Old Stars are the original Angels who were created before mankind. Whenever an Angel is seen as corrupt in God's eyes, they are cast down from the Kingdom of Eden to Earth for a second chance. Others, whose sins are far greater, are not given a second chance. Instead, they are cast down into the flames of Hell as Demons, who are ruled by one fallen

Old Star. New Stars, like myself, Dimitri, Vlad, Rogue and Michael . . . we're a different breed. We were created . . . two hundred years ago. We had the power to walk the Earth amongst humans as guardians whenever we desired and didn't need wings like Old Stars to get to where we wanted. But when we broke the rules and used our powers for selfish gain, God banished us from the Kingdom, along with our powers. Without our powers, although we don't age, we can be killed," he explained as he gazed at me intently for a reaction.

I took a long, deep breath after hearing every word that was said.

"I always knew there was something . . . different about you," I began. "But I never imagined it would be this. Now that I know . . ."

"It's OK. I understand."

"No. I don't think you do. I didn't think it was possible, but now that I know, I am even more drawn to you."

Adrian was clearly taken aback by my response.

"You maybe someone who has fallen, but I too have fallen . . . madly in love. You are my Angel, always and forever."

Adrian was both surprised and ecstatic at my response.

"How do I come into all of this, though?"

"After we lost our powers, we took refuge in this mansion, after Dimitri killed the owners in cold blood . . . the real Runes. Although I hated God for banishing me, I didn't agree with Dimitri killing innocents. Michael also didn't agree, but he chose to find his own refuge. Not long after losing our powers, rumours of a prophecy began to unfold amongst other New Stars. Dimitri found out the full content of the prophecy, but has never revealed it fully to me. He doesn't trust me."

"What did he reveal?"

"On a night of the Black Moon, a child will be born out of Sin but will hold a pure heart. A key she will become in her 25th year to unlocking the gates of Hell . . ."

A wave of panic washed over me. I didn't want to be the key. I didn't want to be the reason for unleashing damnation into the world.

"Remember I mentioned earlier that a fallen Old Star is ruling Hell. His name is Lucifer. Powers cannot be taken away from an Old Star, not even by God himself. Old Stars can only be cursed or banished, but in Hell, their powers are not strong enough to unlock the gates. By unlocking the gates and setting Lucifer free, he has promised his loyal servants to give them all powers once more. As much as I want my powers back, I don't want Lucifer to be released."

"And I won't be unlocking any gates. I'm not going to be the cause for this world's destruction, so it's fine. What else did the prophecy say?"

"*Three sins she must willingly make to darken her pure heart.* I only know of one of the sins. Love," said Adrian.

"*Love?* How is love a sin?"

"It is a sin to love a fallen. This is why Dimitri wanted Rogue to make you fall for him. It's why I showed you hatred so that I could scare you away. But unexpectedly, I grew closer to you. I don't know the rest of the prophecy. I wish I did."

"Well, we will need to find out . . . somehow . . . before I end up destroying this world. What about my mother?" I continued to explain to Adrian all of the dreams I had been having.

"I'm not sure how Ink knows your mother, Sophia. But your dream only seems to support the fact that you were born on a night of the Black Moon."

Chapter 12: The Hidden Room

That afternoon, within its silence, the mansion was quilted with an unpleasant atmosphere. I never even noticed how acquainted I had become with it. Taking advantage of the fact that Dimitri, Vlad and Rogue were nowhere to be seen, I had gathered Adrian, Michael and Raven together in the library.

Raven was perched on Michael's lap and had a pleasant glow about her, almost as though she was a whole new woman.

As she gently fondled Michael's hair, a bemused Adrian was sat in front of them looking rather awkward. Even Taboo looked bored as he lay beside Adrian's feet with his paws stretched out, gazing towards the cylinder bookshelf.

"Hey!" said Raven as she noticed me walk in. The other two turned their heads towards my direction.

"So, why have you gathered us all in here?" asked Michael.

"I have some news," I began slowly. "Adrian has told me all he knows about the prophecy. After completing three sins, it appears I become to key to unlocking Hell's gates. I have no idea how, but . . . it's what has been foretold." I had already known Michael had revealed everything to Raven, as she had confided in me before I had rounded everyone up. Surprisingly, she seemed to have taken it all very well.

"I have already marked off the first sin; falling in love with a Fallen. We don't know what the other two sins are . . . and I can't stay here any longer to allow anymore to be marked off." Adrian looked at me intently. Taboo was pacing around the cylinder bookshelf behind them. I took in a deep breath. "I need to leave you all."

"No, you won't be safe on your own," advised Raven.

"I will come with you," said Adrian.

"We all will," Michael included.

"No. No one will be coming with me. As I don't know what the remaining sins are, I don't want to give anyone a reason to harm any of you in order to get to me.

"Sophia," Adrian started as he stood in front of me, "I made a promise that I will do everything I can to protect you no matter what. I never break a promise, and I sure as hell intend to keep this one. I don't care what you say, I go wherever you go."

"Meow . . . Meow . . ." I looked over at Taboo, who was scratching the wood at the bottom of the bookshelf and peering under.

"What is it, Taboo?" asked Raven.

He continued to meow and scratch away at the wood with his tiny claws.

I strolled up to him and looked underneath to see what he was looking at. There was a small loose piece of wood. As I pulled it towards me, I found a round, black button behind it. Curious as to what it did, I pushed the button. Suddenly, the floor began to shake.

"What's going on?" said Michael, looking around nervously.

The bookshelf began to slowly descend. We watched it descend all the way down until it was no longer visible. A powerful stench wafted upward, making my stomach churn. As we peered down, we could see a narrow, spiral stone staircase leading the way.

"It looks like a secret passage. I never knew we had this," said Adrian, who wore a frown. Just outside the library, the sound of a closing door in the hallway could be heard. "They're back."

"I'm going down," I said, bouncing on my feet.

"Michael and I will go first. We don't know what's down there," explained Adrian.

Michael and Adrian walked down the steps, and Raven and I followed behind. It was cold and dismal down below, but patches of dried, stained blood were visible on the stone walls. We followed the blood stains through an archway, which led towards a room at the end of the tunnel. The closer we got, the more intense the smell became, and as we reached the room, Raven had suddenly turned away and vomited on the floor.

To my horror, I found myself staring at two decaying bodies of a man and woman. Their eyes had been plucked out and their throats had been sliced open carelessly.

"Mr and Mrs Rune. The real ones," Adrian said in low, furious tone. "Dimitri had said he had given them a quick death and disposed of their bodies . . ."

"They were innocent . . ." whispered Michael.

I felt sick to my stomach. Innocents were murdered . . . murdered because of me. How many more were going to die?

"Look, there's something sticking out from his neck," said Michael as he walked towards the lifeless, cold body of Mr Rune. Michael pulled out a small, ancient-looking scroll and unravelled the parchment before reading it.

"What is it?" asked Raven.

"It's . . . it's the Prophecy," Michael gasped. Without hesitation, I pinched the scroll from Michael's grasp, anxious to read what was written.

"What does it say, Sophia?" Adrian asked.

"On the night of the Black Moon, a child shall be born out of sin. On her twenty-fifth year, three sins she will make to darken her pure heart, making her the Key."

I looked up hesitantly, glancing at the others before continuing to read on.

"She will willingly love a Fallen. She will willingly lose her innocence to a Fallen. She will willingly sacrifice her life . . . therefore, becoming the Key." Silence filled the room.

"What?" muttered Adrian.

"No, wait. There is a flaw in this prophecy. They need me to *willingly* sacrifice myself. Well, I'm never going to do that."

A look of great concern washed over Adrian's face.

"Sophia, promise me now. No matter what happens, you won't do it. You'll save yourself first." He spoke firmly.

"Do what? What do you mean, Adrian?" But before he could even respond, voices from behind us made me jump out of my skin.

"Well, well, well. We must have missed our invite!" I had never heard Dimitri sound so joyful until now.

Rogue and Vlad stood on either side of him, each with a glint of evil in their eyes.

Adrian and Michael shifted in front of Raven and me as a barrier.

"Don't come any closer. Let us walk away from here now and I'll save you from your faces becoming distorted," Adrian said in a menacing, low tone.

"Why on God's earth would we allow any of you to walk away?" Rogue said as he cackled.

"Sophia, you know you cannot change what has already been written. This is *your* destiny," Dimitri explained whilst slowly moving closer towards me.

Adrian moved in front of Dimitri, facing up to him and glaring into his eyes.

"I won't do it, Dimitri!" I shouted. "No matter what. You won't be able to make me, either. The prophecy clearly says I have to *willingly* kill myself, which I have no intention of doing. Not today, not tomorrow, not ever!"

"Oh, but you see . . . you will do just the very thing. GET HER!"

Vlad and Rogue rushed towards me.

Within a flash, a bloody fight had broken out between the men as they all began to sink their firm fists into one another.

"Raven, come!" I gestured, running back out through the tunnel.

However, Dimitri had spotted us escaping and followed after us.

We had managed to reach the stone spiral steps leading out, but as we reached the last few, Dimitri had grabbed onto my ankle.

"Come here!" He yanked me down.

Raven, being ahead of me, was out of the tunnel and grabbed onto my arm to stop me from falling.

I kicked Dimitri hard in the face with enough force to throw him back down the stairs.

"Come on!" Raven ushered me outside.

We sprinted out of the library, through the double doors of the mansion and out into the cold, foggy open air.

"We'll have to take Michael's car. I still have his keys thankfully. Come."

But I hesitated as I glanced back at the mansion, embracing the aching pain filling my heart.

"Sophia, Adrian will be fine. They both will, I know it. But it's you they're after. Right now, keeping you safe is all that matters." Even through her words, I could still sense the sadness she felt for leaving Michael.

Raven hurriedly sat behind the wheel as I jumped in the passenger's seat behind. She sped the car around on the gravel path before driving towards the black iron gates.

I looked out through the back window at the mansion, tears rolling down my face.

I didn't want this to be goodbye.

Chapter 13: Sanctus Terra

It was almost dark. We had been driving for some time now. I never even asked where we were heading until the land around me began to appear familiar.

"Is this . . ."

"Your village, Sanctus Terra," Raven completed.

"But why here?"

"Because it all makes sense! I asked Michael why all these events seemed to have only unfolded after you left home and arrived at the mansion. He explained that when you were still living in this village, you were under some sort of shield. Sanctus Terra . . . it's Latin for 'holy ground'. That's why I've brought you back here, because this is where you'll be safe."

"But I no longer have my house. It was repossessed," I confirmed, looking slightly confused.

"Adrian bought the house back for you. He did it a while ago . . . He told me to keep it a secret. He was planning on surprising you one day."

A heavy weight slowly crushed my heart. Every inch of me wanted nothing more than to be back with him again, within his firm embrace. I hoped he was alive and safe.

Driving through the small village, we finally reached the cottage I grew up in. There were only four other cottages nearby. My cottage was tucked away nicely, with a view of the woods far ahead, giving you a sense of privacy and security. It was one of the things I loved most about it.

I opened the front wooden gate and looked around. The grass was overgrown and the proud tree that blossomed every summer now stood bare. Compared to the mansion, my home was miniscule, but I preferred it that way.

I opened the unlocked front door. There was almost a ghostly atmosphere about the place; a home that was once filled with love and laughter now lay bare in darkness. Objects in the lounge had gathered dust, and silver strings of cobwebs had formed in the corners of the room.

I found a pack of matches and lit a candle, illuminating the room, after a quick flick of the light switch showed no power to the cottage. A photo frame still perched on top of the rustic cabinet, just as I had left it. I picked it up and stared at the beautiful woman in the photo: my mother. How I wished she was here to comfort me. To tell me that everything was going to be all right. I wish I never sent her away that day. A silent tear rolled down my cheek.

"She would have been really proud of you, you know," Raven began softly as she placed her arm over my shoulder. "I never had the chance to know my real parents. They gave me up as a child . . . I grew up in an orphanage before I was adopted."

"Oh . . . Raven, I'm sorry. I never knew . . ."

"Don't be silly. Its's fine. It was a long time ago. But what I wouldn't give to be able to even have a fraction of the love your mother gave you. Your mother may no longer be here, but you were blessed to have had her for as long as you did. Now she'll be in the Kingdom of Eden; she is at peace." She smiled.

More tears trickled down my face. I knew she was right, but I still selfishly wanted her back. I had lost my father, my mother, and I was now terrified I would also lose Adrian. I wiped away my tears and took a deep breath. "So . . . what's the plan now?"

"We stay here until Michael and Adrian come."

"But how do you know—"

"They will come. I know it." Her words were strong, yet her eyes spoke differently.

A few hours had passed by whilst we waited restlessly in front of the glowing fire. I had gotten up and paced through the whole of the cottage numerous times, waiting and expecting the worst.

As I stared into the dancing flames for a moment, the wooden cabinet caught my attention in the corner of my eye. Remembering what was inside, I opened the cabinet and pulled out a beautiful, well-kept violin.

"It was my father's. About the only thing I had of him. Mother taught me how to play as a child after she always caught me trying to sneak it away." I laughed as I reminisced.

"Play something," Raven asked softly as she smiled. I paused for a moment, thinking, before proceeding to rest the bow on its strings.

"Come now, child, dry your tears. For when you awake, you shall have no fears.

Fire and Stone are in your soul. True love you will know will make you whole."

"Who taught you that?" asked Raven with a faint frown across her forehead.

"My mother. It was her lullaby to me."

"Interesting words . . ."

"Yeah, it's kind of random, I know. But it's . . . comforting."

Raven simply smiled as the fire began to distinguish.

"Wait here, I'll go fetch some more wood for the fireplace near the trees," I said.

"No. I'll go. You stay inside, you can't risk it."

I nodded as Raven walked outside to gather the wood, but when fifteen minutes had passed, I began to worry. I walked up to the front door and rested my fingers on the door handle, but just as soon as I did so, I heard an all too familiar voice.

"Sssophia, Sssophia . . ."

Of course, there was no one there, and, by now, I had grown accustomed to it. But I didn't like the fact that I was hearing it now of all times. I sensed danger.

I took a sharp knife from the kitchen, tucked it in the back pocket of my jeans and proceeded to open the front door. Looking around the cold, dark surroundings, it was strangely quiet; more quiet than usual. I didn't like it.

"Raven?"

There was no response. Just an echo of silence.

My hands began to sweat and my heart raced as I walked up to the wooden gate and looked around. "Raven?"

Still, there was no response. However, in the distance, at the very entrance of the woods, I saw something. Three figures were faintly visible, one with golden hair. My heart summersaulted in my chest. Could it be . . . was it really . . .?

"Adrian?"

Without a second thought, I opened the wooden gate and sprinted towards the woods as fast as I could. Raven was right all along. They made it out alive! As I continued the pace, adrenaline flowing through me, I slowed down as I neared. The excitement that had washed over me quickly turned into shock as my heart crushed a hundred times over. I stopped, frozen to the spot as I looked ahead. Tears flew from my eyes, and a mixture of sadness and rage swirled at what I saw ahead.

"NOOO!" I cried out. "How could you? She had nothing to do with this! She didn't do anything to anyone!"

Raven's body was nailed to a tree by her hands and feet, her face brutally distorted and covered in blood.

Rogue and Vlad both stood beside her lifeless body proudly, as though they had just won a trophy.

"She was too weak anyway," said Vlad in a cold tone. "She was irrelevant."

"We did her a favour really," Rogue began. "We showed her mercy by offering to give her a quick death. All she had to do was scream out loud, and you would come running out. But annoyingly, she was a stubborn one. Even when we took turns throwing stones at her face, the most she did was cry. Pathetic."

"Stop it . . . please . . . It hurts!" Vlad mocked.

My eyes were fixed on Raven, but my insides burned with rage. I wanted them dead. I sprinted towards Rogue, who stood there smiling and unfazed. Once I got close enough, I pulled the blade out of my back pocket and attacked.

Rogue unfortunately managed to dodge the worst, yet I did manage to leave a long gash across his face. I tried to attack again, but he grabbed my wrist and yanked the blade from my grasp.

"Your end is near, and I will rejoice hearing of your suffering when you go straight to Hell," he spat, gripping me by the hair.

"I won't be going anywhere . . . I won't give you what you want!"

"Yes . . . we will see about that," he said, and with that, he pushed my head into a tree, knocking me out senseless.

Once again, everything became dark.

Mother was running through Sanctus Terra towards the cottage. She was carrying something small wrapped in a blanket. She appeared frightened, and all the while, she continued to glance behind her every so often, as though she was running from something. Eventually, she reached the cottage and locked the door as soon as she was inside. She removed some of the blanket, revealing a baby. Becoming suddenly overwhelmed, she broke down crying. She cried intensely, yet the whole time she held on to the baby firmly. The baby remained silent, looking at its mother with such curious brown eyes.

The room began to fade.

The child was now five: a girl with long brunette hair. She sat in front of a birthday cake that had no candles, just the words 'Happy 5th Birthday Sophia' iced on.

"Mummy, can't we light candles this year?"

"No sweetheart, you know Mummy doesn't like lighting candles." I lowered my sad eyes slowly. "But who needs candles when you have this yummy, yummy cake that Mummy baked, hey? I think I might eat it all by myself!" said Mother, opening her mouth pretending to do so.

"No, Mummy no!" We laughed together whilst Mother began to cut out a slice of cake.

The room faded.

I was now in my teens.

"I don't understand what she had to ground me for! I have never skipped school before, it was just a one-time thing," I told myself as I paced the room. "Stupid school . . . with its stupid bullies. Well, if I'm grounded, I'm not going to sit here alone in the freezing cold." I walked out of the cottage and returned with some wood. "It's about time we lit this fireplace."

The room was now aglow with the crackling fire.

I sat in front of it peacefully, watching the flames as it comforted and warmed me.

However, Mother had just returned home. She took one look at the fire and looked terrified. She ran into the kitchen and returned with a bucket of water and threw it into the fireplace, drowning the flames.

"Mother!" I shouted.

Mother, through her anger, slapped me across the face, but just as soon as she did, her face filled with regret. "Sophia, love, I'm so sorry, I didn't mean—"

But I didn't wait for her to finish her sentence, as I was now storming off to my bedroom. Mother sat in front of the extinguished fire, tears streaming down her cheeks.

I had almost cried myself to sleep. In my half-conscious state, I heard Mother's lullaby being sung to me. Mother always sang it to me when I would cry at night. It made me feel calm again as I drifted off to sleep. Just then, the bedroom door opened slowly. Mother stood in the doorway, looking around nervously. I remained asleep.

"Please, if you're here, leave my Sophia alone. She is mine . . . She is mine," said Mother.

In return, there was nothing but silence.

Chapter 14: Inside the Locked Room

I peeled open my eyes and looked around, taking in the new surroundings as I did so. I was in what appeared to be a dungeon; a cold, stone room all alone. I was still fully clothed, but my wrists were chained up to the mattress I laid on. I pulled and tugged on the chains hard to free myself as my skin burned raw, but it was useless. I ran my fingers through my scalp and felt dried blood, and, suddenly, I remembered how I ended up here as it all came flooding back like a tsunami.

Just as I began to think of an escape, the dungeon door floor open.

"I see you're awake," said Rogue, closing the door behind him. The blood from the gash on his face had dried around the wound.

"Let me go, Rogue!"

"But I thought you wanted to visit the locked room of the mansion. You know, the one you believed was a storage room. Hahaha. Don't worry, you will be free soon enough from this prison . . . *you* call earth."

"I swear to God, I'll—"

"Hahahaha! I pity you humans. Do you really think God gives a damn about you? Look at your life, Sophia. You tell me, where is your God? Your parents are dead, your friend is dead and, soon, so shall your precious Adrian."

"Adrian? Is he . . . Where is he?" I asked as I regained a slight amount of hope in my soul.

"It should have been me you had fallen for. I was nothing but kind to you, yet you were fixated on *him*," muttered Rogue. He came closer and sat on the mattress beside me.

I wrapped my arms around my knees protectively, terrified of what he would do to me.

"I won't lie, knowing he got to have you first made me very jealous. So naturally, it gave me great pleasure beating him senseless."

I didn't know whether to cry or to become consumed with rage. *How dare he hurt my Adrian!*

Rogue began to stroke my face with his finger before I slapped him hard across the face with the back of my chained hands.

"Do you know what Hell will be like for girls like you? No? Well, there aren't enough words to describe the terror that awaits in all its beauty. But what I can say is you will be stripped of your freedom, your happiness and your self-respect. You will become Lucifer's *whore*; one he will generously share with other demons. You will be raped . . . over and over again. You will want it to end and you will beg for death. Only, you will already be dead and a slave of Hell for eternity. That is all that will become of you. It is inevitable. Yet I will do you this one kindness." He looked at me with a devilish smirk before licking his lips. I glared back at him through untrusting eyes. "To ease you into your new world, I . . . will rape you first."

His sinister words echoed through my ears as fear swept over my body.

Rogue grabbed me by the neck and threw me across the mattress on my front. He yanked down my jeans and underwear.

I kicked and struggled hard to escape the weight of his body on top of me. "Rogue . . . please!"

Rogue continued to tear off the rest of my clothing, leaving me exposed and vulnerable.

"Scream for me, you little slut," he whispered in my ear. "I want to hear your pain."

But before he could do anything, the dungeon doors swung open.

I shifted as far back as the chains would allow, holding onto my trembling knees.

"Time to go," ordered Vlad.

"Can't it wait?" Rogue groaned.

"No, it can't. Dimitri's orders." He strolled up to me and began to unlock the chains around my wrists. The back of his hand brushed my skin and, in doing so, made me flinch. "Don't worry. You're not my type." He smirked. After he released me from my chains, he threw my clothes into my arms, gesturing me to get changed.

Rogue's lip curled.

Once I had hastily thrown on my clothes, Vlad gripped my arm in a vice-like grip, ushering me alongside him.

As we exited through the dungeon door, we came into another room. I looked up, wide-eyed. Lying on the stone floor was Michael, barely conscious and dark blood oozing form his scalp.

"Michael!" I ran up to him and gave him a huge hug. "Oh, Michael, what have they done to you? This is all because of me, I'm so sorry."

"Sophia, I'm so happy you're alive," he responded weakly. "Where . . . is Raven?"

I didn't respond to his question. I had no idea how. Unfortunately, I didn't even have a chance to tell him gently.

"Your little girlfriend is dead, Michael," Dimitri answered as he walked into the room with Rogue.

"What . . . NO . . . You're lying!"

"Why would I lie? Ask Sophia, she witnessed her bloody face after my two boys stoned her to death."

Rogue and Vlad both smirked proudly.

My heart was breaking for Michael. I saw his eyes well up with tears. Michael looked at me questioningly.

I simply nodded in silence to confirm.

"All three of you will die a slow and painful death, I promise you!" said Michael in a menacing tone, almost as if a fire had rekindled inside.

"You won't be around much longer, so don't make promises you can't keep, boy." Dimitri stood there, viciously smiling.

Michael eased himself up to his feet. Enraged, he tried to take a swing at Dimitri, but he missed.

With a hard, swift blow, Dimitri swung his fist into Michael's face, throwing him straight back to the floor, unconscious again.

"Now, let us move on, shall we! Sophia, dear, any idea what is behind these curtains?"

For the first time since being in the room, I noticed the long, black curtains drawn closed in a circular shape. But I had no idea what lay behind them.

"What lies behind these curtains is your destiny. Do you understand how special you are, Sophia? You have been *chosen* to set our Lord Lucifer free. In return, he has decided to honour your body by ensuring no other Demon lays a finger on you. Only he will have this glorious right. You will be a prize, his bride, if you like, forever waiting for him to visit you in Hell."

"How very generous of him," I responded, sarcasm lacing my voice. "I'm afraid I'll have to refuse his kind offer because I'm not going to die. Not today."

Dimitri's lips curled. "I thought you would say that." He began to pull down on the chunky red rope that dangled beside the curtains.

The curtains slowly opened, and, as they did so, my heart stopped beating.

"ADRIAN!" I screamed out. Adrian was barely conscious and covered in blood in a tall chair. His arms were stretched by chains that clasped his wrists. Three daggers that resembled crystal shards of glass were unexplainably hovering and pointing towards his face. Two were pointed to either side of his face and the other pointed above his skull. They were all inches from touching him. A crystal-looking ball hovered beside him.

"Uh, uh, uh, I wouldn't touch him if I were you," said Dimitri.

"What . . . what have you done to him?"

"This machine is an old friend of mine. *The Executor*. Its power can only be activated by certain blood. Luckily for us, your blood seemed to be approved. Every two minutes, the crystal shards will move closer towards destroying the beautiful face of your boyfriend. The top one will ensure he has a slow and agonising death. But you can save him. *You* can help him, and I will stand by as you do."

"You would never allow me to save him! Your promises are empty words, Dimitri."

"On our Lord Lucifer's soul, I will not stop you," he declared in a firm tone and looking serious.

"How? How do I save him? Show me!"

Dimitri began to walk towards the crystal looking ball. "The beauty of this machine is its mystery," he said softly as he gazed at the ball in awe. "This ball, called *Vamp*, has the power to start and stop the crystal shards pointing at Adrian. It can only be activated . . . and deactivated by certain blood. Luckily for Adrian, your blood is worthy enough to stop this machine."

"Sophia," whispered a weak Adrian.

"Yes, I'm right here, Adrian."

"Sophia . . . don't . . . do it . . ."

"I can't let you die. I won't. I can save you with my blood—"

"No, Sophia—"

"Listen to me. I love you. I am going to save you, no matter what you say. It only needs some of my blood. After that, you, Michael, and I, can all leave this place." I turned back towards Dimitri, conscious of how little time we had left. "You have to let them both go. Michael and Adrian, and you have to allow them to take back Raven's body."

"You have my word, on Lord Lucifer's soul."

"Then I'm ready . . . What do I have to do?"

"You must pour your blood onto the Vamp," he said as he pointed to the crystal ball. "As you slowly feed it your blood, the shards will begin to retract." Dimitri walked towards me and pulled out a sharp gold knife from inside his jacket and offered it to me.

I stared at the knife for a brief moment before confidently taking it from his grasp. "How will I know—?"

"When it will be enough? You will know."

"Sophia, don't!" shouted Michael, who was regaining consciousness.

Rogue and Vlad stood either side of him, ensuring he didn't get in the way.

"I have to, Michael. I can't let him die . . . I can't let either of you die." Without waiting a moment longer, I took a deep breath and carefully sliced my right wrist. It was painful, but I didn't care. The blood began to flow out from my fresh wound and onto the Vamp.

As my blood poured onto it, it disappeared as if it were being absorbed. A sharp pressure began to drain my blood faster, as though the ball was sucking the blood from my wrist.

The shards moved back a few inches from Adrian.

Relief flooded me.

I continued, the whole time looking at Adrian. Tears fell from my eyes as a realisation slowly settled in.

This is it . . . This is my end. The end of any hope of being with Adrian.

"Sophia," whispered Adrian, sitting above me, "if you do this, you will lose your place in Eden. Opening the portal, the gates to Hell . . . God will consider this a great sin. You will burn in Hell, Sophia. I don't want that for you. Please . . . stop . . ."

More tears poured down my face as my blood continued to be sucked out of my veins. "I know, and I'm ok with that . . . I will follow any path you follow, remember? I am choosing you . . . I love you Adrian . . . I'm ready to burn for you."

The shards had almost moved six inches away from Adrian now, and I began to feel weak as my vision blurred.

"Michael, have Raven buried in Sanctus Terra. Her body will be protected there. My home is her home after all."

Michael nodded as his eyes filled with tears.

"Adrian, my love. You were right about one thing. It seems we were never meant to be together." I could feel his heart crushing along with mine.

"Please . . . don't go . . ." he whispered as tears fell down his beautiful face.

"I have to . . . I'm sorry." The room darkened around me.

A few moments later, the crystal shards were fully retracted and the room trembled and crumbled in slow motion.

"Adrian, I . . ."

The chains around his wrists finally loosened and fell to the floor, setting him free. The Vamp had had its fill. Adrian jumped out of the seat and secured me in his arms as I fell into them.

I felt his tears fall onto my skin.

"Sophia . . . what have you done? Stay with me . . ."

"Rogue, take the Vamp!" ordered Dimitri. "I don't understand what's happening . . . The Portal is . . . being moved."

"Adrian, I . . . I . . ."

"Yes?"

But I was never able to finish. All the muscles within my body relaxed, and I stilled as the last gasp of air left my body.

Chapter 15: Epilogue

The sun was beginning to set, a blanket of amber light sweeping over a grave in Holuny Woods that Michael sat next to. He held a bunch of beautiful blue roses, which he lay gently on top of the grave.

"Normally, every month he would send red roses. He said they were a symbol of the fire and beauty you held. But this time, he sends blue. He still hopes that there was a chance you would have gone to Eden instead of Hell . . . We both do. I told him to come and visit you. But like always, he chooses not to." Michael breathed in the spring air and looked around. "It's strange how the silence of Holuny Woods can bring out its beauty. It's why we buried Raven here, too. I know what you asked, but she wouldn't have wanted to be in Sanctus Terra alone. She would have wanted to be with you."

Michael stood and stared at the grave. "I pray that God took mercy on your soul."

"What if he didn't need to?" said a voice from behind him.

Michael spun around to find someone unexpected. A tall, slender man with one ear who bore an ugly scar across the side of his left face.

"What are you doing here, Ink?" Michael groaned.

"You ought to be a little more careful. It's not safe hanging around all alone. You never know who might be lurking within the woods," chuckled Ink.

Michael, through his rage, wrapped his fingers around Ink's neck firmly. "Cut your bullshit, Ink, and tell me what you want."

"Ahh, there is . . . really no need for that. Especially . . . as we are both on the same side," he choked.

Michael loosened his grip, pushing Ink away. "What do you mean?"

"I tried to ensure the prophecy wasn't fulfilled. Sophia had to lose her virginity to a Fallen, willingly, which is why I tried to take it by force . . . It would have ensured the prophecy remained unfulfilled."

"What a pathetic excuse. You tried to rape her, end of story! And why did *you*, out of all people, want the prophecy to remain unfulfilled? That would mean you didn't want Lucifer released."

"Lucifer will be released sooner or later. Dimitri and the others already have an idea of the new location of the Portal, so it's only a matter of time. But that is not the reason I wanted the prophecy unfulfilled. It's not why I am fearful." Ink's gaze moved and rested on the grave. "I'm going to share a story with you—"

"Ink, I don't have time for your games."

"But you will listen, for we are all running out of time."

Michael glared at Ink for a moment before gesturing him to continue.

"There was once a happily married human couple. A man and a woman. Yet the woman had an invisible void within her that she couldn't fulfil; a baby, due to her infertility. Out of desperation, she made an agreement. An unbreakable contract. She would have a baby, but in return she would have to sell her soul."

"To Lucifer?" asked Michael.

"To Lilith. She agreed to this, yet she never truly understood the heavy price of her request. On the night of the Black Moon, twenty-five years ago, she tried to change her mind but was told it was too late. The deal had been signed by blood. She was told her husband was already there. She was taken into the woods . . . here. Holuny

Woods. She saw the ring of fire and who was within it. Her husband. He lay between the flames on a bed of twigs, naked as the great Goddess Lilith rode on top of him, fulfilling her sexual needs. He was completely under her trance, obeying her, enjoying her. The poor woman's heart was crushed. She cried and screamed out, but her screams were ignored. Once Lilith had taken the seed she needed from the man, the man was engulfed in flames, burning him to ashes. Within seconds, Lilith was able to grow a child within her and give birth to it. She was a beautiful girl. Sophia Stone."

"That . . . can't be . . ." Michael whispered. "Lilith is cursed. She cannot have a child that will live past the age of—"

"One. Yes, if she slept with a demon . . . but the man, Carlos, was human."

"How do you know all this?"

"My father was present that night. Aamon Blackcrest. Before he was killed, he told me this story, and so I dug deeper to find out more."

So . . . you're saying . . . Sophia is—"

"A demi-god: the offspring of a Goddess and human. The blood of Lilith flows through her veins, meaning she is immortal, a Princess of the Night. Yet she is a new breed . . . The first of her kind. She is the second part of the prophecy. You see, pursuing the three sins awakened the other half of Sophia, her demon side. Her soul simply needed to be corrupted, and she needed to *willingly* sin so that she is no longer pure of heart."

"So, what does this all mean . . . Is . . . is Sophia alive?" asked Michael, who looked astonished by what he was hearing.

"She never died. Not physically anyway. Half of her soul has darkened. When she awakes . . . she may not seem the same. With everything that had happened to her, everyone one who had hurt her, she will bring with her a rage like wildfire. Her rage will be the key to defeating Lucifer. Sophia is . . . the second most powerful being after God himself. That . . . is what I am afraid of. She must be taught the art of balance."

"So . . . she has half a soul left that is still pure . . . that is still Sophia. What will happen if that, too, darkens?"

"Then . . . I will say something I never thought I would say. God help us all."